Life and Life Only

Life and Life Only

Dave Moyer

iUniverse, Inc.
New York Bloomington

iUniverse books may be ordered through booksellers or by contacting:

iUniverse
1663 Liberty Drive
Bloomington, IN 47403
www.iuniverse.com
1-800-Authors (1-800-288-4677)

ISBN: 978-1-4401-5462-1 (sc)
ISBN: 978-1-4401-5460-7 (dj)
ISBN: 978-1-4401-5461-4 (ebook)

Printed in the United States of America

iUniverse rev. date: 07/22/2009

Moyer takes the reader on a sweeping journey chronicling the losses and victories of Dan Mason and his family. Paired with the songs of Bob Dylan, the narrative in *Life and Life Only* is a window, a vision, into contemporary American life.

- Nate Jordon
Founder and President of Monkey Puzzle Press

Moyer's *Life and Life Only* goes well beyond a simple following inside the life and love of baseball pitcher Dan Mason and his journey into manhood. It is easy to realize and transpose many of these same actual truths and adventures with real life examples. The storyline is more than believable; rather it is replayed in actuality over and over again with real players in real places. Moyer does a wonderful job of keeping parallel the timeline of Dan Mason's career in conjunction with actual events of the country which further identifies the reality of the times. The real truth is that Moyer intersects the paths of fiction and non-fiction time and time again in a highly believable manner. It is a must read for any baseball fan who can appreciate the trials and tribulations of a player searching for two loves."

- Carl Moesche
Area Scout, Major League Scouting Bureau

For all who played and all who loved.

So don't fear if you hear
A foreign sound to your ear
And it's alright, Ma, I can make it . . .

And if my thought-dreams could be seen
They'd probably put my head in a guillotine
But it's alright, Ma, it's life, and life only.

--Bob Dylan

It's Alright Ma (I'm Only Bleeding)

Chapter 1

Oh, where have you been, my blue-eyed son? . . .

Oh, what did you see, my blue-eyed son? . . .
And what did you hear, my darling young one? . . .
Oh, who did you meet, my blue-eyed son?. . .
I met a young girl, she gave me a rainbow . . .

Oh, what'll you do now, my blue-eyed son?. . .

--Bob Dylan
A Hard Rain's A-Gonna Fall

Dan Mason entered the world in 1974, the same year that Bob Dylan reunited with The Band for the first time since their blistering tour of England in 1966. They opened up at the old Chicago Stadium on January 3rd. Tickets for the two-night stand sold out in less than a half-hour. A fortunate twenty-four-year-old, Don Mason, Dan's father, managed to score tickets. During this seminal tour, Bob regularly performed the song "It's Alright, Ma (I'm Only Bleeding)", and scowled the lines, "But even the president of the United States/Sometimes must have/To stand naked." Later that year, President Richard Nixon, embroiled in the Watergate scandal, announced he would resign rather than face impeachment.

Dan was born into the chaos of the 1970s. In addition to Watergate, America witnessed the Saigon airlift on television—an episode that became the country's final image of the scar that would not heal. America discovered that free love led to a multitude of divorces. Gas prices rose, and the country endured a brutal recession. The Iran hostage crisis and the subsequent bungled rescue attempt horrified the nation. All of this occurred before Dan could sufficiently color between the lines.

Don and his wife Emma accepted the challenge of starting a life together and raising a family during this turbulent decade. Don met Emma McBride at Northern Illinois University. They bumped into each other in line at the bookstore when they were buying their books for the fall semester of their junior year. She was in line ahead of him, and according to Don's version of the story, the incident was not an accident. Dan always recalled his father's hardy laugh whenever he told the story.

"Excuse me," Don said to her, somewhat abruptly.

"It's okay. You must be in a hurry," Emma said.

"Not really, but if you leave the store too quickly, I will be in a hurry to catch up with you. Wait for me. I'll carry your books back for you—to make up for my indiscretion."

Don impressed Emma as supremely confident. He possessed humor and charm and had a certain presence about him. Emma was taken by him at their initial encounter, but in one very unique way, they could not have been more opposite. Outwardly gregarious, Don exuded a type of robust fortitude. He retained the south-side Chicago toughness of his ancestors, but on the inside, he was not as comfortable with himself or as confident as he wanted others to think. He wanted to emerge on top in any encounter, and, early in his childhood, basketball became his vehicle to channel this need. Emma, on the other hand, was meek and somewhat shy in social settings. She would often reach for the right word in conversation and feel like she hadn't expressed herself as she intended. Emma was not naïve. In the bookstore encounter, as in most situations, she knew the score. She matched Don equally in street smarts, but Emma possessed a great gift. She did not feel the need to have to continually prove herself. She could keep her composure and let life's disappointments go before they built up to destroy her. However, on the inside, she was pure and elemental and became the rock and the center around which their family would be built. When she became pregnant with Dan, she took a deep breath and considered the world around her and decided that under no circumstances would she let any of it impact her family. They would not become a casualty of the times. Emma developed a bitter resolve to insulate them from all the utter nonsense that engulfed them. In so doing, though a woman of few faults, she missed many opportunities to let her humanity crack through that thick shell.

A wealthy town, Barrington, Illinois, rests along the old Northwest Highway, Route 14, about thirty-five miles northwest of Chicago. Don's great-great grandfather had migrated to Chicago, and his offspring had worked in the steel mills, stockyards, and packing houses on the south side—wherever they could find work. His children and grandchildren had gradually moved farther away from the city as their circumstances had improved—a common occurrence in most families—and eventually, Don settled in Barrington with Emma.

Don and Emma graduated from college in 1971. Don got a job as a math teacher and freshman basketball coach at Barrington High School and rented an apartment in town. Don enjoyed a solid high school basketball career. He could shoot but possessed average ball-handling skills. He grew to be exactly six-feet tall. Even back then, he was too slow to guard anybody and too small to play shooting guard in any major program. His heart, desire, and work ethic were not enough to overcome his lack of size, speed, and quickness. Rather than play college basketball at a small school, he went to Northern. From the outset, he intended to become a high school teacher and, eventually, a head basketball coach. Ultimately, he aspired to be a college basketball coach.

Prior to getting married, Don had converted to Catholicism to keep the peace. Emma lived in McHenry with her parents that first year out of school. She worked as a nurse at Good Shepherd Hospital in Barrington. McHenry, a blue collar town about twenty-five minutes northwest of the affluent suburb of Barrington, contrasted sharply with the community she would soon call home. Emma's Catholicism did not prevent her from making excuses to stay with Don in Barrington as often as she could manage, during bad weather or at times when she worked late. Technically, she would join him permanently in June of 1972, following their wedding at St. Patrick's Church in McHenry.

Dan inherited the confusion of the times in his very constitution, and he would never quite make sense of it. Dan developed a restless soul and became easily agitated. He felt a deep need to accomplish things to prove to the world it couldn't conquer him. His parents fueled the fire. They expected success and drove him to it. He developed the belief that he could never let them down. When he had something on his mind, he rarely felt confident sharing it with them, for fear of that look of dismay that either or both often shot his way. Finally, Dan just stopped volunteering information. He didn't know his parents were doing their best to do what they thought was right, and they didn't know what the proper parental thing might be any more than they understood how their expectations impacted Dan's perception of his place in the world. They were shooting in the dark.

While the Masons did the best they could to provide a solid foundation for their future lives together, Gerald Ford, who had pardoned Nixon, stood no chance for re-election, and Jimmy Carter, the Governor of Georgia, became president of the United States. The hostage crisis and massive inflation doomed his presidency, and, with the help of Jerry Falwell's Moral Majority, Ronald Reagan became the country's fourth president in seven years.

People were scared. Dan was Don and Emma's beloved oldest son, and they took comfort in his achievements. If Dan excelled, then everything must be all right, despite what the evening news might be telling them.

Throughout all of the unrest, Bob Dylan continued to record and perform. In 1975, Dylan released *Blood on the Tracks*, containing, among other songs, "Tangled up in Blue", "Simple Twist of Fate", and "If You See Her, Say Hello". In 1976, he released *Desire*, his first number-one album. In 1979, he released *Slow Train Coming*, the first of his three religious albums. Dylan won his first Grammy for the album's opening song, "Gotta Serve Somebody".

Don and Emma struggled to make ends meet in the pricey suburb. No matter how much Dan noticed his clothes were different from the other kids', no matter how tight his basketball shoes were, or how raggedy his glove became, Dan never suggested that he wanted different clothes or needed new equipment unless his mom or his dad initiated the conversation. His brother Dylan, three years his junior, had it slightly worse. Though perhaps less common in Barrington than other places, people of that era routinely handed down clothes to their same-sex younger siblings, and Dylan often ran around the neighborhood and attended school in ill-fitted clothing. Emma balanced the checkbook to the penny, scolded Don when he charged items, and had 100 different uses for leftovers. Dan and Dylan never complained. It's not that they didn't want to. They learned very early on that complaining did no good. In that day, children were still spanked. Just as the boys had learned to take off their shoes immediately upon entering the house, just as they had learned to put their dirty laundry in the basket before it hit the floor, so too did they learn not to complain about the food that Emma served them.

Don became the head basketball coach at Barrington High School, and by the time Dan and Dylan would play for him in the late Eighties and early Nineties, the enrollment had topped 2,500 students. An incredibly driven man, Don threw himself into the job, attending clinics and working summer camps all over the place, trying desperately to secure a college coaching position. While Don ran a widely respected and enormously successful program, Emma took on the role of healer—the voice of reason. However, frequently left on her own with Dan and his brother, she often had no choice but to play the "heavy," while Don, who was not noted for his patience or tolerance, was the "hero." When Don returned home and stormed through the front door on his white horse, his boys flocked to him. Don, the successful basketball coach and town hero, was *their* dad!

A classic coach's kid, Dan grew up in the gym in the winter and in dugouts each summer. His mind was a computer, processing the action and rarely, if ever, missing anything that happened on the floor or on the field. His dad took him to practices and games. When they watched a game on television together, Don explained each and every nuance to his son. It wasn't long before the roles were reversed and Dan took the lead, correctly interpreting the action that was occurring, causing his dad to remark one time that he would make a great color analyst someday.

Dan entered the third grade at Hough Street Elementary School around the same time that Reagan took office. Dylan had just released *Shot of Love*, the third of the trilogy of religious albums, containing the masterpiece "Every Grain of Sand". With Dylan entering kindergarten, Emma returned to work. A couple weeks into the school year, Dan, a teacher's dream—a fact that did not go unnoticed by the other children—was falsely accused in an incident at school. One afternoon, a custodian found a cigarette butt in a urinal in the bathroom located in the same wing of the building as Dan's classroom. Passes verified that Dan was indeed one of two students who had used the bathroom that morning, making him a prime suspect. The office secretary called Emma at the hospital, and when she arrived at the school, Dan was called to the office. When Dan entered the office, he saw his mom, dressed in her white nurse's uniform, sitting in a chair in the corner.

Emma stood about five-feet, six inches tall, with dishwater blonde hair that came down and rested ever so lightly on her shoulders. Her narrow, opaque blue eyes featured pupils that centered slightly closer to the nose than the middle of her cheeks. Emma, usually angelic in her patience, was certainly a rookie at visiting the principal's office to discuss her children's behavior. Her discomfort was obvious to Mr. Salvatori, the principal, but not to Dan. She effectively concealed that from him. She had lost her pregnancy weight and looked more like a college nursing student than a mother of two. However, when times demanded it, Emma and her slightly freckled, girlish face were all business, and she transformed herself from nurse to nun. That is the face Dan saw when he entered the room, and it became more typical as the years passed.

Dan immediately grew petrified. He had never been in trouble at school before, but he knew something must be wrong. He had no idea what that might be, but his mom would not be there if everything was okay.

"Mom, why are you here?" a shaking young Dan inquired.

"Dan, sit down," Mr. Salvatori said.

"Mom, what happened?" Dan asked.

"Listen to Mr. Salvatori, Dan. Sit down. It'll be okay," Emma said.

Emma always said, "It'll be okay." Dan thought that had to be her favorite phrase.

"Dan, we found this in the bathroom." Mr. Salvatori held up a cigarette.

"It wasn't me! I don't smoke!" Dan said, fighting back tears. Tears would indicate weakness. Dan did not want to appear weak in front of his mother or let on that he was scared.

"Dan, it had to get there somehow. The only other boy who used the bathroom said he didn't do it. One of you had to do it. Why don't you just tell me what happened?" Mr. Salvatori asked.

"Because I don't know what happened!" That was it. Dan couldn't hold it in any longer, and he began to cry.

Mr. Salvatori continued to ask the same questions in different ways, and Dan continued to deny smoking a cigarette in the bathroom. He condemned smoking, period, managing to expound on the evils of tobacco in the process.

Finally, Emma said, "My son said he didn't do it. I think we're done here. I'm taking him home."

Without official sanction from Mr. Salvatori, Emma got up, put her hand on Dan's shoulder and said, "Come on, Dan. We're leaving."

The next year, Dan had Mrs. Ericks for his fourth grade teacher. The first time Dan asked for a bathroom pass, he discovered that she allowed her class to use the same bathroom he had used the previous year when the incident with the cigarette had occurred. The rules stated that her class should use a different bathroom, but technically, the other one was closer, and, while against school policy, she routinely let her class use it. Mr. Salvatori never did find out how the cigarette butt got into the urinal, but Dan figured out it had to be one of the fourth grade boys from last year who had been responsible. However, that fact could never alter what had happened. Though Dan thought his parents tended to believe him, and while nobody ever proved anything, the element of doubt would always be there. Dan had done nothing wrong but felt he had let them down. It was his teacher who was wrong, but now Dan had to pay the price. Emma had to leave the hospital in her work clothes to come to school when Mr. Salvatori had accused her son of smoking. Her son—also the son of the town's revered basketball coach and a third grader, no less—had been smoking at school. This had been what everyone said, even though it wasn't true. Dan had shamed them.

Never again. No matter how much Don and Emma may have believed in their son over the years, Dan developed the mentality that he must constantly prove himself to them. By his successes, through his steadfast commitment to being the best, by out-achieving everyone, Dan alone could prove his worth and thereby assuage his parents' deepest fears of failure.

As the second child, Don and Emma accepted Dylan for who he was and felt less of a need to drive him. As a result, Dylan developed a much more easy-going personality.

In Dan's later years, when he needed something to soothe his troubled soul, he found solace listening to music, especially the music of Bob Dylan. In addition to chaos and confusion, Dan had also inherited a love for Dylan's music when he had entered the world.

About the time of the bathroom incident, it became obvious to everyone in Barrington that Dan could throw the hell out of a baseball. Dan so overpowered his little league brethren that, on most days, they were lucky to hit a decent foul ball off of him. Dan joined a travel team at age ten. His dominance continued, and, as the hitters got better, he mastered a change-up. He had such good control that, even on days when the opposition managed a few hits here and there, they rarely scored any runs off him. As Dan progressed through middle school and high school, the whispers began: Dan Mason was going to be a big league baseball player.

Barrington suffered from no shortage of attractive girls. By the time Dan had graduated from Barrington High School, he had grown to six-feet, two inches tall. It was the perfect size for a pitcher. Dan had matured into a fine-looking young man. One might be inclined to think a blue-eyed, athletic, straight-laced, all-American boy to be a great catch for any number of girls, but Dan found the concept of girls and anything relating to them very difficult to wrap his head around. Many girls seemed attracted to danger and excitement. Dan, a handsome, straight-"A" student, was going somewhere, but many girls apparently found this too boring. He wanted a pretty girl to like him. Was that asking too much? Yet, as he looked around, many of the prettiest girls were dating losers. Much of the rest of the pool dated older boys. *Why won't a girl like me?*

As Dan grew older, he noticed that his mom became increasingly more irritable. Some kids' moms were making their lunches for them, tending to their cuts and bruises, baking cookies. Emma fulfilled her obligations. She made supper, did the laundry, and made sure their clothes fit, but, outwardly at least, one had to look hard to find the love.

"Did you take your shoes off?"

"Yes, Mom."

"Did you unload the dishwasher?"

"Yes, Mom."

"Did you do your homework?"

"Yes, Mom."

Emma could be very demanding. As Dan tried to figure out what he needed to do to get a girl to like him while simultaneously feeling the need to please his mom, he just became more confused. He couldn't figure out what women wanted, but, like everyone, he wanted to please and he wanted to be liked. The only answer came to Dan in the form of an increased determination to excel at baseball. This, at least, he could control.

Dan had no way of knowing that Emma needed to preserve all of her strength to keep her marriage together, which, to her way of thinking, was in everybody's best interest. Don's dream of becoming a college coach—an uphill climb from the start— had slipped away. He had never played in college, and that limited his connections. But the financial obligations of raising a family in Barrington and ensuring his kids had the opportunity to pursue their dreams meant something had to give. Not surprisingly, Don's dream took a back seat. Though the boys would never realize how big of a blow this had been to their father, he never really got over it. The constant financial pressures, combined with people running in every direction to this ball game or that, made life rather unwieldy in the Mason house. Emma didn't know how people managed to exist before microwaves. Don's demeanor began to deteriorate noticeably. He took to yard work to distract his mind from the reality of his present situation. Dylan knew even less of the once-jovial young man than Dan did. Who knew what Dylan might have been thinking? In their house, it was not something one talked about.

The 1980s came. As Don and Emma tried to keep their family together and raise their boys, Reagan, nicknamed "The Great Communicator," filled the role as president. He had a calming influence on a nation in turmoil and brought the country hope. He became best known as the president who said, "Mr. Gorbachev, tear down this wall!" George Bush, Reagan's Vice President, succeeded him in January of 1989 and, early into his presidency, The Wall fell and the Cold War finally ended.

Reagan advocated for government deregulation, which, while nice in theory, was not without consequences. Michael Milken, the king of high-yield (junk) bonds, was indicted on ninety-eight counts of racketeering and fraud. Charles Keating, Jr., the chairman of Lincoln Savings and Loan, made donations of about $1.3 million to five United States Senators, tabbed "The Keating Five," including Republican John McCain of Arizona, who would one day run for president and lose. Lincoln amassed $135 million of unreported losses and surpassed the regulated direct investments limit of $600 million. The Senate Ethics Committee determined that three of the five senators had substantially and improperly interfered with the Federal Home Loan Lending Board investigation of Lincoln. McCain, a prisoner of war for five years in Vietnam, was cleared of having acted improperly but criticized for having exercised "poor judgment." On Friday, October 13, 1989 (Black Friday), as the decade came to a close, the stock market endured a "mini-crash." The era of the Savings and Loan Crisis, Wall Street greed (see Tom Wolfe's The Bonfire of the Vanities), and junk bonds, ended.

Or, as Bob Dylan also sang in "It's Alright Ma (I'm Only Bleeding)", "While money doesn't talk, it swears."

The 1990s came, and Don and Emma continued to try to keep their family together and raise their boys. Dan entered high school. His parents had no way of knowing how good Dan would become at baseball, and they were very worried about financing college. The strain added lines to Emma's once-angelic face and girth to Don's once taut mid-section.

The Cold War may have "ended," but, as always, there had to be war: this time, Iraq. Bush had inherited the financial debacle, but less than a year later, he had another problem when Saddam Hussein, the ruler of Iraq, invaded oil-rich Kuwait. Allied Forces made a mockery of the Iraqi army. The war was an overwhelming success, and Bush's approval ratings spiked to eighty-nine percent. However, the budget deficit had tripled in the previous decade. Unemployment was increasing, and corporations were reorganizing and laying off workers.

Bush's approval ratings plummeted to a brutal twenty-nine percent, and he would not win re-election.

Dan grew up a tough kid in a soft town. He blocked out all of the turmoil around him: societal and personal, internal and external. He choked down whatever feelings he had and concentrated on exactly two things and two things only. He wanted those two things very badly. He wanted to pitch in the big leagues, and he wanted a pretty girl to unlock the dormant warmth he knew existed in his heart.

The closing song of the opening Tour '74 concert in Chicago on January 3, 1974—the concert Don attended in the year his oldest son was born—was "Most Likely You Go Your Way (and I'll Go Mine)". Nobody knew how prophetic that would turn out to be.

Chapter 2

Well she was an American girl
Raised on promises
She couldn't help thinkin' that there
Was a little more to life
Somewhere else

--Tom Petty
American Girl

"Are you packed and ready to go?" Emma asked Dan.

"I'm packed. I have everything," Dan said.

"Don, are you ready to take Dan? You two need to leave," she hollered out across the house.

"Emma, we have plenty of time," Don hollered back.

"You have to pick up Peter and Kevin, remember?"

"I remember, Emma. I remember."

Dan left the door to his room open, and Don walked in.

"You ready to go?" Don asked him.

"I'm ready."

Dan enjoyed his freshman year of baseball, but he couldn't wait for the summer to come. His travel team entered a tournament in Savannah, Georgia, and all spring, that was all he could think about. Finally, the time had come to load his equipment into his Dad's car.

Dan said goodbye to his mom.

"Well, I'll see you in a week," he said.

"Okay. Don't get hurt."

"Oh, Mom," Dan muttered.

"I'm going to miss you, Dan."

"I'm coming back, Mom. I'm not leaving forever."

Emma knew, one day, he would.

"Did you say goodbye to your brother? You know he hasn't said anything to you, but he's a little upset."

"He'll be fine, Mom. It's one week. I said goodbye."

Now Don became impatient. He had gone out to start the car and walked back into the house.

"Well?" Don said.

"Well, let's go, Dad."

They pulled out of the driveway, picked up Dan's friends, turned on to Route 59, took Interstate 90 East, and, forty-five minutes later, they arrived at O'Hare Airport where they met up with the team at the Delta Terminal.

"See you next week, Dad."

"You excited? You've never been away alone before."

"I'm excited, Dad."

"Sorry, I can't go. You know we have camp this week."

"It's okay, Dad. You have your team to coach. I'll be fine."

"Well, goodbye, son. Play hard."

"I always play hard, Dad."

"Maybe that's because I always remind you."

They laughed awkwardly, neither sure how to say goodbye. They never had to do it before.

Later that evening, Dan arrived in Savannah. The entire experience captivated him: the airport, the plane ride, the bus ride, checking into the hotel—everything. His team had a game every day. Dan performed well all week against excellent competition. He played on perfectly manicured fields in majestic weather for baseball. Dan felt like a big-time ballplayer, almost like he was in "The Show", a common phrase ballplayers used to describe the major leagues.

However, he liked something else almost as much as the baseball. He was old enough to notice that, everywhere he turned, incredible-looking girls surrounded him. The sight of these foreign beauties almost made the palmetto bugs bearable. All of these slim girls moved with natural grace and possessed a manner of speech that Dan found enchanting. He wondered how many times a day they had to wash their hair to get it to look like that. He thought, *God, it's hot down here;*

don't they ever sweat? To Dan, these girls personified perfection. And the accent was more than he could take—the plus after the "A" on a perfect test. That summer—the summer of 1989—Dan decided that if he ever got married, it would be to a southern girl.

Dan returned from Savannah that summer, and with his natural instincts activated, he developed a curiosity as to whether any of the local girls would measure up to what he had just experienced. He secured a date for the Homecoming dance that could best be described as "going through the motions." Tricia, his date, wanted to go to the dance, and so did he. They got along fine and were "seen" at the dance. He awkwardly kissed her goodnight. They talked a few times at school over the next couple weeks, but they never went out again and gradually stopped speaking to each other.

Dan thought he liked a few girls in his classes and tried to talk with them whenever an opportunity presented itself, but most girls took interest in other types of boys. Dan overheard talk of parties and sexual activity that moved well beyond appropriate according to what he had been taught. At the end of his sophomore year, a girl did take an interest in Dan, which he took great joy in. Sheri was very pretty and popular, and Dan felt he had arrived. Things moved quickly, and Dan, unable to handle any of the complexities of the situation lived in a happy state of confusion while trying to keep his grades up and perform on the field.

During the summer Dan came to believe he was actually in love with a girl. In August, the Barrington Broncos opened up their football season at home against Libertyville. Dan and Sheri went to the game. Dan dropped her off at her house after the game and stopped at a gas station to fill up on his way home. He ran into Kevin, one of his friends from the baseball team, who asked him if he was on his way to the big party. Dan tried to brush it off, but Kevin said, "Why don't you come over? You don't have to drink."

Dan knew from signing the athletic code, not to mention his dad's constant badgering, that he could not be at a party where alcohol was served, even if he was not drinking. However, Dan was getting sick and tired of being "Mr. Straight Arrow," so he went. He walked into the house, much to the surprise of everyone there, and descended down the stairs that led into the basement. He turned the corner from the game room where several kids were playing pool to see who was all in the other room, and when he did, he saw Sheri making out with the quarterback of the football team.

Emma's Catholic conscience had been drilled into him, and in his own mind, Dan, for a person his age, had developed a pretty strong sense of right and wrong, and this could not be justified—it was wrong! He stormed out of the room and began to head up the steps when Sheri realized what had happened.

"Dan, Dan, wait," she screamed.

Bitches, bitches, all of them, he thought.

Ten minutes later, Dan walked through his own front door.

Don and Emma were watching television, waiting up for him. Dylan was already in bed.

Immediately Emma noticed something was wrong. "Dan, you okay? You sick? You don't look so good."

"I'm fine, mom. Leave me alone please."

"Dan, tell me what happened."

Dan kept walking to his room.

Don said, "Emma, leave him be. He'll talk when he wants to talk, if he wants to talk. I've seen that look before. There's not one damn thing you can do. Not one."

Dan never said a word to either one of them. Don, of course, learned of the details that week at school. Dan often relied on his mom for comfort, and Don had a difficult choice to make. He chose not to disclose the details to Emma. He could see no reason to upset her in addition to Dan, and thought that there was nothing she actually could do to help Dan feel better. This situation involved a girl, and it was possible, in Don's mind, that if Dan knew that Emma knew, it might make everything worse. It was a judgment call. He may have erred.

Later that week, Don asked Dan, "You, okay there, Dan?"

Dan said, "Yeah, Dad, I'm okay."

So Don let it go at that.

The episode between him and Sheri cemented everything for Dan. Between his mom and the girls at school, he could no longer take the angst that came with women. In his rage, Dan chose to focus completely on his sports. He had confidence in himself on the field and the court. He excelled at sports, particularly baseball, and he could more easily control the outcomes. If he lifted weights, practiced and trained properly, accepted coaching, and competed hard, his natural ability could do the rest, and more often than not, he came out on top. With women, he appeared to have no natural ability to compete, much less come out on top. Yet, despite his current state of disappointment, there was a part of Dan that very badly wanted to think there was a girl out there for him somewhere.

Dan played varsity baseball for three years and started for his dad on the basketball team his junior and senior season. He probably would have been a Division III guard in college, except for one thing. By his senior year in high school, the scouts clocked his fastball at ninety-two miles per hour.

The Detroit Tigers drafted Dan after his senior year in the eighth round. They offered him $14,000 to sign a professional contract. Instead, Dan elected to attend college. College coaches convinced him that, if he developed as they thought he could, he might be a first or second round draft choice in just three years. By then, who knew where the bonuses would be? They went up every year. He could be offered $500,000 to sign. Maybe more. So, with the help of his dad and his baseball coach, Dan tried to sort through his options, which were almost limitless.

Schools in the south featured better college baseball, and that helped him narrow his choices. He wanted a reasonable shot to pitch as a freshman, so he narrowed it down some more. He could major in education anywhere, so that didn't matter. If for some reason things didn't work out, he planned to become a coach—like his dad.

The power conferences in college baseball were the PAC-10, the Big 12, the SEC, and the ACC. He visited some schools and tried to get comfortable with the coaches and decide what campuses he liked. Then, one day, while trying to make sense of everything, more confused than coherent, when all the campuses started to look alike, a single, distant memory flickered for just an instant, and inside his head, Dan heard the sound of southern girls talking. A warm feeling of comfort overtook him, and it all became clear: Dan would attend the University of Georgia. Its head coach, Steve Webber, had been recruiting him heavily. In 1990, Dan's sophomore year in high school, Georgia defeated Oklahoma State University 2-1 to win the College World Series. In 1991, Georgia's record slipped to 27-31, but in 1992, Dan's senior year, Georgia rebounded to a 35-25 won-loss mark and qualified for the NCAA Regional in Tallahassee, Florida. Georgia lost to Kent State 5-2 and to Stanford 7-3, but the program appeared headed in a positive direction.

In August of 1992, Dan became a Georgia Bulldog: a bona fide SEC baseball player. He entered into a dream-world that, for the majority of kids who ever play little league, remains just that—a dream. But it was Dan's reality. He dressed out in Georgia practice gear. Georgia issued him his hat, jacket, travel bag, and other equipment, and he didn't have to fundraise for any of it. The school just gave it to him. He lifted weights in the off-season with other Georgia baseball players, also proudly dressed in Georgia practice gear. People in class knew he was on the Georgia baseball team, and, for twenty-four hours a day, Dan had all he could do to keep from grinning mindlessly from ear to ear. Despite all that, he remained as humble as a college male freshman, wearing Georgia baseball gear and about to embark on a season of SEC baseball could be. He wavered some but, for the most part, maintained a level head. He treated people decently, did his school work, and followed the instructions of his coach.

That spring, Dan did not make the conference rotation. Webber slotted him as the team's fifth pitcher, which meant he would throw the midweek non-conference games and pitch in relief on the weekends in the conference games. Considering all of the starters ahead of him would eventually get drafted, Dan found himself in the same position as many freshmen pitchers in big-time programs. The scouts projected him as a future major league pitcher. Brian Powell, a freshman who did make the conference rotation as the team's third starter that year, posted a 17-5 career record at Georgia, and Detroit, of all teams, picked him in the second round in 1995. Powell would go on to play six years in the big leagues, and there was minimal difference between him and Dan. The pitcher who earned the fourth slot in the rotation that year nudged out Dan solely because he threw left-handed.

Dan had a great season, posting a 4-1 record and a 3.68 earned run average. His most memorable game occurred on April 13th, though he did not appear in the game. Eighteenth-ranked Georgia hosted sixth-ranked Georgia Tech. Three thousand, seven hundred twelve fans jammed Foley Field, whose capacity was listed at 3,291, and saw Georgia Tech defeat Georgia 4-1. It was the eighth largest crowd in school history. Coming off a regional appearance the year before, there were high hopes the Bulldogs, but the team finished the season one game over .500, with a 30-29 record, managing a lowly 10-18 mark in the SEC, albeit arguably the toughest conference in the country.

That summer, Dan pitched for the Springfield Sliders of the Central Illinois Collegiate League, visiting exotic locales such as Danville, Dubois, DuPage, and Quincy. He amassed nine wins against two losses and recorded a meager 1.73 ERA. For that, he was named the CICL pitcher of the year. His parents and younger brother came to see him pitch frequently. The hitters spent the summer adjusting to wood bats, and, for Dan, it all seemed too easy.

In his sophomore year, Dan earned the number two spot in the rotation behind Powell. He threw big game after big game. He and Powell carried their weight, respectively, but the season would be an even greater disappointment than the one before. Georgia's finished the season with a 22-35 record, a pathetic mark to the locals, especially when compared with Georgia Tech's ongoing success atop the ACC. Dan finished with respectable numbers against the tougher conference competition (four wins, five losses, and a 3.48 ERA), capturing every regional scout's attention. The Falmouth Commodores of the Cape Cod League invited Dan to play for them that summer. The Cape Cod League remains the most prestigious summer league around. The best players played there, and all the scouts followed. The Atlantic Ocean and the towns of Bourne, Brewster, Chatham (Powell's team), Cotuit, Harwich, Hyannis, Orleans, Wareham, and Yarmouth-Dennis were more appealing than the prairies of the summer before, to say the least.

Dan had always liked to read and decided to major in English. Over time, he had developed into a bit of a newspaper fiend, and, unlike most of the college kids he hung around with—kids who simply wanted to have a good time and get through school—Dan paid attention to current events. As he was developing into a potential first-round draft choice, the world around him continued to spin.

Bill Clinton and his wife, Hillary, became president in January 1993, amid rumors of an extramarital affair between him and a woman named Jennifer Flowers. Clinton preferred to focus on domestic issues, but he inherited a military conflict in Somalia, and soon, the country would hear stories about ethnic conflict in Bosnia. In February of 1993, one month into his presidency, Islamic extremists, who viewed New York's World Trade Center as the symbol of everything they despised about America, captured the country's attention when they detonated a car bomb below Tower One, killing six and injuring over 1,000 people.

Federal prosecutor Kenneth Starr led a Federal investigation of Clinton's real estate dealings in what became known as the Whitewater Scandal. Newt Gingrich, a Republican Congressman from Georgia, figured prominently in the political controversy of the time. He and Dick Armey of Texas co-authored the Contract with America, taken largely from Reagan's 1985 State of the Union Address. When Congress proposed deep cuts in spending, Clinton, whom conservatives despised, vetoed the budget, and the government shut down. Public sentiment went Clinton's way, further enraging Republicans.

As the budget shut-down came and went and the conflict in Bosnia escalated, Clinton continued to be dogged by personal issues, mostly related to sexual impropriety. Attorney General Janet Reno gave Starr the authority to expand the scope of his investigation, which afforded the country the opportunity to learn about Paula Jones, "that woman" Monica Lewinsky, blue dresses, and the definition of the word "is." Dan's life would explode by the time it had all unraveled and Clinton had managed to narrowly escape impeachment.

Dan considered the first half of 1994 a great time to be alive. That spring, Falmouth invited him to play for them. He followed Woodstock '94, the 25th Anniversary of the original event, which marked what some people called a "comeback" for Bob Dylan. Dan listened to the unbelievable bootleg recordings of that concert repeatedly, but the truth was that Bob had never gone away. However, in the '80s, the general public saw him as a "has been" who became best known for bumbling the Live Aid appearance, "sleepwalking" through concerts, and disguising himself in hooded sweatshirts. Then, in 1988, while touring in Europe, he described an experience where, "It was almost like I heard a voice . . . I am determined to stand whether God will deliver me or not. And all of a sudden everything just exploded . . . After that is when I sort of knew: I've got to go out and play these songs." Dylan continued to perform over 100 shows a year well into the next millennium. No matter what, one has to keep on going, or "keep on keeping on," as Bob sang in "Tangled up in Blue". Dan never forgot the story and heeded the lesson.

About this time, Dan began hearing voices again. He had an education class at Aderhold Hall, located in South Campus, and he overheard a girl named Anna Jean Simpson telling a girl named Betsy, sitting next to her, that she, too, was going to be a teacher. He had been hearing the sound of southern girls talking for almost two years now. But this time, something registered. The irresistible force that had subconsciously drawn him to Georgia in the first place—that seed in a distant alcove of his mind that had been planted almost five years ago—began to germinate.

For the next two weeks, Dan tried to get to class early enough to position himself in just the right place to see Anna Jean, and perhaps even sit beside her. All of his classes had to be in the morning in the spring so he could make his afternoon games and practices. Dan had back-to-back classes, and his English class, which preceded his education class, met at Old School in North Campus, about as far away as one could get from Aderhold Hall. Dan did not dare to skip English because he would most likely have to run until he puked once his coaches found out. Dan tried running to get there faster, but that didn't work. Exhausted and out of breath, the rest of the class seemed mildly amused that this college athlete entered class every day horrifically out of breath. Dan finally gave up. On Friday of his second week of class, he arrived later as he had prior to his track experiment. When he sat down and looked around the room, Anna Jean was not there. She always beat him to class. Maybe she was sick. Hopefully, she didn't drop the class. Dan thought, *Please, not that— anything but that.*

After class the previous Wednesday, Anna Jean, on her way out, had said to Betsy, "Watch this."

"What do you mean?" Betsy had said.

"Watch me when I come to class on Friday," Anna Jean had said.

So, on Friday, Betsy watched the door out of the corner of her eye. Dan, meanwhile, stared compulsively in the same direction. Finally, just before class the professor stepped up to podium, Anna Jean appeared and gracefully entered the room. She had seen all she needed to see, and she had made up her own mind about Dan. She walked past her traditional seat, glanced at Betsy, and . . . sat down right next to Dan.

Dan knew nothing of what went on in class that day. His mind drifted to unknown places. His stomach jumped around inside his chest, bouncing off his ribs, falling through the seat of the desk, repeating the process over and over. He had never been such a nervous wreck. *Don't screw it up—don't screw it up,* was all he could think. The torture ended fifty minutes later. Shortly after the professor said his final words for the day, Anna Jean leaned over, and softly, near Dan's ear, in that voice, she said, "Since you couldn't get here any earlier, I decided I would come a little later." With that, the deal was sealed.

Dan, transformed into a glob of Jell-O, almost fell to the floor as he tried to get out of his desk. He mumbled, inaudibly, "I guess I'll see you on Monday."

"I'm sorry. I didn't understand you. What did you say?"

And then, Dan just figured, *What the hell? I've gotten out of bases-loaded jams before, and this is a bases-loaded jam. And when I did, it was because I mustered up the courage to fight the good fight. Not because I served up some half-assed pitch, hoping to get lucky.*

Dan stood up tall, composed himself, and said, "Anna Jean, if you are available, would it be possible to get together some time this weekend?"

"Why, I think I'd like that."

Later that day, Dan called his dad.

"Dad, I have a date with this great girl tomorrow night."

Trying not to completely crush his son's obvious enthusiasm, Don said, "Son, there's a lot on the line for you. Be careful." And then, out of duty, he added futilely, "I'd hate to see you get in over your head."

But Don knew it was already too late. He had coached his son all those years, and his son had listened to him. Still, he knew there were some things one could teach a person, and some things he had to learn for himself.

Dan lived in student housing with his teammate, Billy Sinatro, who was also a pitcher. Anna Jean, a sophomore by credit, was a year older than Dan. She had transferred to the University of Georgia after her freshman year, when she had attended East Georgia College in Swainsboro. Not all of her credits had transferred. However, having spent one year in the dorm, she decided it would be preferable to live off-campus.

On Saturday night, Dan stopped by Anna Jean's apartment around five-thirty. Anna Jean greeted him at the door, and Dan stood in silence, completely amazed. He had seen her in class every day, and blinded by his daydreaming, she was about all he saw, but to be at her apartment and see what he saw another thing entirely. Dan usually stared at Anna Jean's face, and she did not need make-up. She often came to class dressed plainly, but on this night, Dan saw her as drop-dead gorgeous without the slightest hint of being flashy. Something about what she had done with her make-up made her deep brown eyes stand out even more. She did her hair slightly differently, too, but Dan, awestruck, couldn't distinguish any particular changes. He just knew he liked what he saw. Then he noticed her jeans. He had never seen jeans look like that on anyone before. He didn't think anyone should be allowed to sell them. *They're just jeans*, he thought, but then he thought, *No they're not. They're Anna Jean's jeans. That's why they're different!* A light-weight sweater adorned her upper half and clung perfectly to her. Standing about five-feet seven inches, Anna Jean was rather tall. Together, they were about as handsome a couple imaginable. Dan had all he could do to gain some semblance of composure.

They considered trying to get into one of the college bars. She had turned twenty-one, but Dan had not and did not want to jeopardize his status on the baseball team. So, they went out for pizza at Gumby's. Anna Jean drove.

They settled in and ordered some soft drinks and garlic cheese bread for an appetizer, and then, Dan took it upon himself to begin the conversation. He tried to be a good listener that evening, so as not to appear too full of himself. He could, after all, listen to that voice for hours on end and never tire of it. Still, he could not help feeling like he was talking too much.

"So where are you from?" Dan asked.

"Swainsboro. It's called 'Crossroads of the Great South,'" Anna Jean said.

"Is it in Georgia?"

"Yes. It's at the intersection of Highways 1 and 80. A lot of other roads cross there, too. That's why they call it that. It's, like, halfway between here and Savannah."

"I never heard of it, but the first time I was in Georgia, I played baseball in Savannah. I liked it."

"I've heard Savannah's nice. I've never been there."

"Well, maybe we can do something about that someday. How many people live in Swanisboro?"

"Oh, about 7,000."

She asked him questions, too, like why he had come to Georgia. He chose not to tell her he was drawn to Georgia by a voice that he now believed was hers. He thought that might be a bit much.

"I wanted to play baseball down south," Dan said.

"Why?"

Anna Jean knew he played baseball, but she didn't know anything about baseball and didn't pretend to. This didn't bother Dan in the least. He was not interested in Anna Jean for her baseball acumen.

"The baseball is better down here. There are more scouts. I wanted to improve my position in the draft," he said.

"So scouts draft you, I take it, and then what?"

"Then I play minor league baseball for a while, and if I'm good enough, I get to play in the major leagues."

"So you think you're going to play in the major leagues?"

"The Tigers thought so when they drafted me out of high school. If I stay healthy, I think I can do it."

"You were already drafted?"

"Yep."

"Well, what are you doing here?"

He skipped the part about the voices, and before he could catch himself, he said, "They offered me $14,000 in the eighth round. If I go in the first round next year, I might get as much as $500,000 just to sign," and then, realizing what he had just done, looked down, somewhat ashamed. Dan had mastered that emotion. What had gotten into him? All he wanted was for her to like him, but he had gone too far.

Anna Jean almost gagged, but then she saw the look on Dan's face as he looked at his shoes and said, "I suppose big leaguers have to date pretty girls. I was First Runner Up of the 1988 Junior Miss Pine Tree Festival Pageant, you know."

"I didn't," Dan blurted out. "How the hell didn't you win?"

She smiled. *He's cute*, she thought.

The waitress, another college student, brought them their pizza. It was a thin crust pizza, with sausage and onions on Dan's half, and pepperoni on Anna Jean's half. Dan hoped someday he could take her out for real pizza, Chicago-style, like Gino's East or Lou Malnati's.

Anna Jean continued with her story.

"Swainsboro has its big annual Pine Tree Festival. It goes all the way back to 1946. The Kiwanis Club sponsors it, and my dad was the chairman of the organizing committee. They have a 5K run, bike ride, lawnmower races, golf tournament, tractor show, Civil War reenactment, lumberjack show, a parade, all that stuff. Some people think the judges didn't vote for me because they thought it would look bad. My dad was really proud of me anyway. After the pageant, someone took a picture of us. I still had my banner on. He was smiling the biggest smile I've ever seen."

"You know, I don't think that's right. If you earned it, you earned it."

"Maybe on our way back from Savannah some time, we could stop in Swainsboro and go to the festival?"

She was hinting at a future.

"Okay by me!"

Then Dan started over. "So, what else about your dad? What does he do?"

"He used to work at the Swainsboro Sawmill for Rayonier Wood Products. Shortly after the pageant, he died in a car accident."

Anna Jean explained that he had been driving on one of those rural roads that converged on Swainsboro, Highway 4, and had lost control of his car. There were no other vehicles involved, no sign of an animal crossing the road, no inclement weather, no alcohol—nothing. It was, near as anyone could tell, a fluke accident— as random as Dan being in Georgia for a baseball tournament and hearing voices, and as random as he and Anna Jean being in the same class. The Swainsboro *Forest Blade* called it "the most tragic occurrence in Emmanuel County in recent history." The article described Eugene Simpson as an upstanding, hard-working pillar of the community, who regularly attended the First United Methodist Church.

"That must have been really hard. I'm sorry."

"It's okay."

A few moments passed. Then Dan asked, "So, you go to the First United Methodist Church?" Dan could see this being a problem someday.

"I used to go every Sunday with my mother when I lived at home. Back when my dad was around, we were more of a 'family,' and we all went to church together, including Joey—he's my brother."

One time, years later, when Dan visited Swainsboro, he looked in a phone directory and learned there were ten churches in Swainsboro, none of them Catholic.

"Was it hard on Joey?" Dan asked rather stupidly, as it obviously must have been.

"I guess. He never went back to college," she said.

"What does he do now?"

"He took dad's job at the mill."

Over time, Dan pieced the story together the best he could. Nobody ever talked about it around him. From what he could figure, Joey, a running back in high school, attended Georgia Tech on a football scholarship his freshman year in college with the understanding he would be moved to safety. When he chose not to return, rumors were rampant. Why would such a promising athlete and hometown football hero drop out? Others wondered if he was too depressed about the accident. No one ever found out that his grades were marginal. Still, he was eligible to return. Joey, unlike his sister, had more of a nose for trouble. Some speculated he had some trouble with the coaches, or that he drank too much once he went off to school. His behavior after the death of his father did nothing to quell the rumors of an undisciplined lifestyle, but what preceded what? Did the drinking lead to him dropping out? Did the accident lead to the drinking? Nobody knew. Joey did his job at the sawmill during the day and went out with his buddies at night. He never hurt anybody in the process. He also never put any money away, never left Swainsboro, nor ever appeared to aspire to anything at all.

A year later, as Anna Jean entered her final year of high school, Joey moved out of the house. While Eugene worked at the sawmill to support his family, attended church, and was active in the community, Joey worked at the sawmill for no apparent reason other than to pay his rent and afford to go out with his buddies, who were no more motivated than him.

Dan tried not to be too judgmental. He also had pondered the eventuality of his father's passing and did not know how he would be able manage that loss. Death, by definition, is the absence of life, and therefore a tragedy, no matter what the circumstances. How could a person know how he would behave in the face of tragedy? Anna Jean, the youngest child and only girl, her daddy's sweetheart, seemed relatively accepting and matter-of-fact as she chronicled her father's death and the present circumstances that had brought her to the University of Georgia and, for that matter, pizza with Dan at Gumby's.

Dan tried to move the conversation in a different direction. "So, why did you decide to come to Georgia?" Dan asked.

"Well, when my dad died, my mom took a desk job in the Registrar's Office at East Georgia College. I went there as a freshman to save money. But Joey was becoming a problem, and my mom and I both thought it would be good to look to transfer. I had good grades and everything, and I just felt the need to get out of Swainsboro. I wanted to see something else, see what was out there. For being the 'Crossroads of the Great South,' there's not much that goes on in Swainsboro," she said.

"Well, that makes sense," Dan said.

"My mom wanted me to be the first one in the family to graduate from college." Louise, Anna Jean's mom, didn't want her to be trapped in Swainsboro any more than Anna Jean could find a reason to stay.

Later that night, they drove back to her apartment and had a couple of beers. Dan saw the picture of her and her father that she mentioned at Gumby's sitting on the TV stand. In a wicker basket to the side of the television sat the banner, draped over a few magazines and some books.

Dan learned a great deal that night. He learned much about Anna Jean. He realized other people had dreams, too. He also discovered that he liked kissing Anna Jean. Though ill-adept at navigating such complicated terrain, he also thought that Anna Jean liked him.

The spring of 1994 consisted of a feeling-out process between the two. Baseball kept Dan away quite a bit, and, when home, he had to make sure he was up to speed with his studies. Of course, Dan could not help but find plenty of time for Anna Jean, but in her opinion, she ranked second in the hierarchy behind baseball. She accepted this, but tension invariably crept in at times.

Anna Jean supported Dan. She came to all of his starts. She made some friends with some of the other guys' girlfriends. The guys chided Dan in a manner that demonstrated their approval. "You look a little tired today," etc. "And your schedule tonight, Dan? You're pitching tomorrow, if you remember." "Dan, were you born with that smile on your face, or is that a recent phenomenon?" They got on Dan more about being a Yankee and the way he talked than anything else. But no one ever crossed the line because they liked him. He was a good teammate and gave them everything he had. He was, among other things, and maybe above all else, dependable.

For some reason, Anna Jean did not seem comfortable with Dan visiting Swainsboro just yet (most likely Joey), but Louise came up for a weekend once when the team was home to meet Dan, and very much approved of him.

Dan visited Anna Jean's apartment frequently. Usually, her roommate, Cynthia, was there, but not always. Sometimes Betsy came by with some other friends. Dan's teammates Brian and Billy stopped by on occasion, as well. They went to house parties on occasion and hung out at Gumby's with the team after games. Had he known many details, Don would have been comfortable with the pace of things. They danced a strange dance, both burning in each other's absence, but cool in person, as if each was afraid to scare the other away.

Then, after the disappointing season mercifully came to a close, Dan left for the Cape. Dan and Anna Jean made plans for her to visit toward the end of June, after he settled into his apartment and knew his way around the area a bit.

The Cape Cod League season started in mid-June, after the College World Series ended. Dan pitched, completed his workout in between starts, and traveled around on buses with a bunch of other guys. The routine didn't vary much from any other team he played on.

Still, Dan reveled in the camaraderie. Maybe they all got along so well because they knew after a couple weeks they'd be done with each other, but similar goals and experiences bonded these ballplayers together, and they enjoyed each other's company.

When the schedule allowed, Dan and his teammates went to a couple Red Sox games at Fenway Park, a perk of his journey to the Cape.

Emma called regularly for updates.

"Did you do anything exciting this week, Dan?" she would ask.

"I threw pretty well Tuesday against Brewster. We won a close one, three to two," he replied.

"Stop teasing me like that, Dan. You do that every time. Save that for your dad. He can fill me in. You know I'm not talking about baseball. Tell me about Boston. Tell me about your experiences."

Emma couldn't wait until the following week, when their family planned to visit Dan. She missed her son, who had been away for a long time, and couldn't wait to see Boston. No detail was too obscure to share. She wanted to know everything. Dan enjoyed this version of his mom but experienced it all too infrequently.

Dan told her about the Boston Tea Party Ship and Museum, the Paul Revere House, and the Old North Church. He tried to tell her these stories with the same flair that his Irish uncles might, but he knew he fell short.

"I'm saving the Irish Heritage Trail for your visit," Dan told his mom.

Emma was so proud of her son. There was nothing that he had shared with her about his summer at the Cape that was not common knowledge to the entire staff of Good Shepherd Hospital and the majority of patients who came through the door. She felt infinitely more comfortable bragging on Dan around her colleagues and strangers than telling him directly that she was proud of him or, for that matter, actually loved him.

Dan and his cronies drank plenty of beer. One time, Dan hooked up with Brian, and they talked about how much they were looking forward to the next season. There were high hopes for the Bulldogs, with the two of them at the top of the rotation. Players had to be careful not to develop too much of a negative reputation, which some did, as it might hurt when the scouts talked among themselves. Dan prepared himself for every start and didn't get too crazy, but he did stretch his limits farther than he ever had before. Some of the guys spent a significant portion of the summer in a haze. Dan would not take it to that extreme.

Dan enjoyed some of the auxiliary benefits of his good fortune. Not everyone was blessed with the talent that allowed him to experience various areas of the country essentially for free. Dan had seen the Southeast, and now he was summering in the Cape. He did not want to take anything for granted. He breathed it all in. He did not partake in extracurriculars with women, though this was prevalent, and Dan found the way some girls shamelessly threw themselves at ballplayers a little more than reckless. In fact, though some would consider it "normal" behavior on the part of these ballplayers, Dan found it a bit troubling that the majority of his brethren displayed a complete lack of self-control in this regard.

Dan was not naïve. He had seen this behavior as far back as high school and certainly at Georgia, but the extent of it and the complete lack of discretion bothered him. It just didn't seem right.

One time, when he called his dad, he alluded to this.

"Dad, you should see these girls throw themselves at us. I was in the bullpen the other day, and one of them flashed her crotch at me right in the middle of an inning. It's out of control."

"You just figured this out now?" his dad asked.

"Well, I guess I kind of knew it was like this. But I guess I didn't realize it was this extreme."

"The sooner you get used to it, the better. You need to be very cautious, Dan. One mistake, and you could throw everything you worked for right out the window."

Dan was a bit perplexed that this information did not surprise his dad in the least.

Watching this behavior for two straight weeks made him long for Anna Jean's arrival even more.

To say that Dan was excited when Anna Jean arrived would be the equivalent of a fisherman's excitement when a muskie bites. Muskie come up to the surface to feed only at certain times, certain water temperatures—the conditions have to be ideal. Selecting the perfect bait under given circumstances is very tricky. The thrill of the bite of a muskie is one of the most exhilarating moments imaginable. Reeling it in is an even greater challenge. Muskie fishing is a sport. Fisherman throw these fish back until they catch only the finest, and then they keep it and mount it. Dan's muskie, the biggest fish in the pond—or at least she was to him—was now seeking him out. He valued her, and certainly did not really consider her a game or a fish, but the analogy made sense to him.

Unlike throwing a baseball, this quest was unnatural to him. It made him uncomfortable and unsure of himself, but something inside him told him he must keep going. Dan's two dreams converged on him. He was on the brink of pitching in the big leagues and dating the First Runner Up in the Miss Pine Tree Festival Junior Pageant of Swainsboro, Georgia (and she should have won it), and she undoubtedly would have been the real Miss Pine Tree Festival Pageant Queen someday, had misfortune not stepped in. Anna Jean's association between the event and the untimely loss of her father made it too painful for her to consider running again.

Finally, on a Friday morning at the end of June, Dan got in his car and drove up Highway 6, went over the bridge, got on Pilgrims Highway until it hooked up with I-93, took the Ted Williams Tunnel to the turnpike and, an hour-and-a-half later, arrived at Logan International Airport. Ted Williams, former Red Sox great, once said, when he walked down the street, he wanted people to say, "There goes the greatest hitter who ever lived." He achieved his dream. Williams, an Air Force fighter pilot, possessed spectacular vision. Despite missing five years of his prime to two different wars, Williams, the last hitter to bat .400, finished his career with 511 home runs and a .344 lifetime average. Dan thought it was very cool to be able to say he had driven through this tunnel.

Forty-five minutes later, Anna Jean's plane landed. She was happy to see Dan, but she was tired.

"How was your first flight?" Dan asked.

"Well, it took off early enough this morning," she said

She had to take an early flight to make sure Dan had plenty of time to get back to that evening's game.

"Was that necessary? I don't make the game schedule."

Dan tried his best to ignore any baseball commentary from Anna Jean. He did not want to hear it, so he chose not to. They dropped her bags off at Dan's apartment, relaxed for a short period of time, and then headed over to the ballpark.

After the game, they returned to Dan's apartment. He had made arrangements for his roommate to stay with another teammate for the weekend. Players took this type of thing for granted and routinely extended and returned favors in these matters.

Soon after, Dan and Anna Jean shared each other's gifts often and with great intensity and variety. Where this came from—the stories they had heard, the things they had read, the movies they had watched, the experiences they might have had prior—did not matter. Their lovemaking seemed driven by a shared subconscious, as if they mutually engaged in these behaviors with no deliberate thought. What happened that weekend was only between the two of them, and would always only be between the two of them. The origin of their attraction—the mystery of nature and humanity itself that manifests itself in our world without explanation—this enigma that exists to perpetuate the species is, in fact, responsible for some of life's most disastrous decisions. This thing between a man and a woman overtakes reason, for surely human reason cannot be so faulty as to lead one to consciously behave and think as he does when under this spell. It must be that people simply cannot help themselves against nature, for they are a part of it.

In summary, Dan and Anna Jean were quite happy to see each other. None of what happened that weekend seemed in any way wrong. In fact, it could not have seemed more right. Dan felt less confused. There was no logical explanation why he needed to spend an intimate evening with her to feel this way, but that was the affect it had on him. Dan felt more relaxed and confident. A girl finally liked him, he thought, and he wondered if just maybe, he had finally inched one step closer to becoming a man.

That morning, when Anna Jean caught her first glimpse of Dan walking around the apartment, she realized she had never woken up alone in the same house with Dan before. His piercing blue eyes sparkled like she had never seen before. Walking around in his T-shirt, he cut the image of Stanley Kowalski from *A Streetcar Named Desire*. At that precise moment, she was overcome with him—he was all man. She adored him. A lucky man has one moment in his life when he does not have to feign confidence, and, for Dan, this was that precise moment. Most get to experience it once. An unfortunate irony accompanies this experience, however. Because men typically lack the intuitive sense to know what is happening, they not only cannot enjoy the moment, but they cannot replicate it, either. Only an outside observer can sense it, like at a family gathering when gossipy aunts peer at young lovers and say, "Look at those two, so in love."

Dan was scheduled to pitch on Saturday. After the game, Anna Jean said, "Dan, you didn't pitch very well today. Is something wrong?" She actually seemed legitimately concerned.

"Not at all. Just a rough outing," Dan said, quietly laughing to himself.

Dan threw the ball well that summer. He finished the season with a 5-2 record and a 2.34 ERA. His velocity peaked at ninety-four miles per hour, and he could throw all three of his pitches for strikes. At the end of the season, his velocity dropped a bit, which caused some concern, but everyone attributed it to a "tired" arm that simply required a little rest. They shut him down for the last week of the season as a precaution. One more season of college baseball, and he would again be eligible for the draft.

Dan was in love. He had the world by the tail. He had the best time playing ball he'd ever had. He felt that a girl liked him—loved him. Dan enjoyed the best summer of his life, but, unfortunately, he would never have another summer like it. Dan did not yet know the cruel reality for all athletes: all the best in life is left behind at a very young age for these young men. Much is given to them at a young age, and most of their accomplishments occur well before the age of thirty.

Their athletic prowess cannot be replicated as they grow old, and they must leave behind their dreams and fondest memories, making it difficult for many to plow ahead through the future with seemingly little to look forward to. Many resort to living in the past while the present and future pass them by. For Dan, the best was already behind him. Dan found himself, among other things, in over his head.

Chapter 3

I wanna rock and roll all night
And party every day
Rock and Roll All Night

--Kiss
Rock andRroll All Night

Dan would not have pitched well the weekend of Anna Jean's visit regardless, but something was very wrong.

Dan spent most of the fall of 1994 either hooked up to electric stimulation machines or undergoing ultrasound treatments. The Georgia coaches agreed with the people at Falmouth to shut Dan down at the end of the summer, but when he began working out again in the fall, they were concerned that his velocity was not topping out at ninety-four miles per hour, where it had been, but rather hovered in the eighty-eight to ninety range. Dan appeared to be "pushing" the ball, and his fastball had lost some "life". He'd "lost a foot" on his fastball. In baseball lingo, these phrases described more than decreased velocity. They referred to the absence of that late, hard movement on the ball, which is the essence of what actually gets hitters out.

Dan had no idea what had happened. He felt a dull thud in his shoulder, but recalled no specific injury. Everyone speculated that Falmouth overused Dan, but they didn't. Managers in the Cape were very delicate with pitchers. No manager could withstand the reputation of wrecking one of these kids' arms. Each of these players theoretically had bright futures and incredible paydays awaiting them in a very short period of time. If anything, Georgia might have overused Dan the previous spring, but in their mind, they hadn't.

When Dan's arm first seemed "dead", like most pitchers, he tried to pitch through it. Sometimes pitchers go through a "dead arm period", other times they suffer a little tendonitis, and if it lingers a week or two, they simply skip a start and are fine. Dan told his pitching coach at Falmouth as soon as he noticed the irregularity, and they handled it appropriately. Nobody thought it necessary to panic.

When Dan did not improve with treatment, the Georgia trainers referred him to Dr. Chandler, the Atlanta Braves team doctor, as a "precaution". An MRI revealed a torn labrum. Dan required surgery. When he got the verdict, Dan went back to his place, picked up the phone, and called home. Anna Jean sat next to him with her hand on his shoulder.

"Hello?" Dylan answered the phone.

"Hi, Dylan."

"Hey, Dan, how're you doing? Practice going okay?"

"I've been better. Can you put Dad on?"

"Sure, Dan. You don't sound too good. You okay? Anna Jean okay?"

"Yeah, will you get Dad!?" Dan snapped.

"It's okay, Dan. It's okay. Settle down," Anna Jean whispered softly.

"Okay. Take it easy. He's right here," Dylan said.

Dylan turned around and handed the phone to his dad.

"It's Dan. He doesn't sound too good."

Don took the phone.

"Hey, big fella. Something wrong?" his dad asked.

Dan choked back the tears, unsuccessfully trying to keep his dad from hearing him cry.

"Well, Dad, I'm . . . well, it's like this. I'm not good. I can't pitch." Dan had defined himself by this ability for the past twelve years. He feared his dream might be coming to a crashing halt.

"Can't pitch, eh? Well, how long are you out? They going to have you rehab for a couple months, I suppose, and be ready to go January?"

"It's worse than that, Dad. It's a torn labrum. I need surgery. It's already scheduled for next week. I'm out for the year."

"Dan, it's a tough break. There's nothing any of us can do. You have to try to accept it."

"I don't know what to do, Dad. It's my whole life, shot to hell."

"Maybe not, Dan. People come back. Everything is very advanced now. Who looked at it?"

"A bunch of people. I can't remember them all. Then they sent me to see the Braves' doctor. He said, for the extent of the tear, there's a less than fifty-percent chance I could throw at all this season. It's not an elbow, dad. It's a shoulder. Dad, I'm scared."

Anna Jean was trying to calm him down.

"Dan, I'm going to put your mom on."

"Emma, get in here! Emma!"

Emma came immediately. Though Dan and his mom frequently battled, when Dan really needed somebody, he turned to his mom, and Don knew it.

"Don, what's going on?"

"Dan's on the phone. He's scheduled for shoulder surgery next week. He's very upset. He needs his mom."

Dan overheard this through the phone. *At least I only have to say it once,* he thought.

"Dan, it's mom. Dan, it'll be okay. It will. It'll be okay. Is Anna Jean there?"

"She's here."

"Don't let her go anywhere until you calm down, and call me tonight, anytime—it doesn't matter. It's going to be okay."

Anna Jean hadn't planned to go anywhere that night, but if she had tried to leave, she would not have been able to get past Dan. Now, it was Dan who had been the victim of a random act.

Dan spent the entire year rehabbing. The doctors and trainers expressed confidence that he could begin to throw again over the summer. Everyone expected Dan to recover and be ready his senior year.

Dan's mood bordered on depression after the surgery. Rehab exhausted him. Every day he had to do his prescribed resistance exercises. He underwent electric stimulation and ultrasound treatments, started to lift weights to build up strength, and the entire time worked his legs with heavy weights and ran and rode the machines to maintain his cardiovascular endurance. January proved to be particularly difficult for Dan. While he sweated in the training room for hours a day with no apparent end in sight, the rest of the Bulldogs prepared for the season. Prognosticators predicted Georgia would rebound from their disappointing 1994 season. However, with only Powell at the top of the rotation to go with a bunch of young kids, it managed a 29-29 overall record, but finished a brutal 9-17 in the SEC.

Anna Jean supported Dan terrifically. Together constantly, they developed an easy rapport with each other. Anna Jean seemed more relaxed than she had the previous spring. Dan didn't travel with the team, and without the constant pressures and time commitment of the baseball season, she seemed more comfortable in their relationship. Dan felt more like a normal college student, and that helped cushion the blow of the injury.

Dan's wallet contained several pictures of Anna Jean, but very little cash. Anna Jean worked over the summer, while Dan was in the Cape, and had a part time job at school, and she willingly carried him on more than one occasion.

One night, Anna Jean noticed Dan seemed particularly down. "Want to go to the Nowhere Bar tonight?" she asked.

"You buying?"

"Don't I always?"

"Not always. But I will give you that one," Dan said.

They laughed. They laughed a lot that spring.

They hung out at the Nowhere Bar when they wanted to watch sports on TV. It had over 100 types of bottled and tap beer. Dan decided he might as well be a normal college student for that one spring, and like everything else he did, he gave it his all. Dan believed that by the time he had left Athens, he had sampled all of the Nowhere Bar's offerings. Dan and Anna Jean met the team on occasion after games. They never felt rushed and savored the love they felt for each other.

A skeptic might question if Anna Jean truly loved Dan, or if she had ulterior motives, such as security or a lingering hope for a big payday. Dan never gave it a thought. When she said she loved him, he believed her. She probably did, or thought she did. When one is happy, one doesn't ask too many questions. Dan had a pretty girl on his arm. He enjoyed what he had for what it was. He could see no reason not to trust what his heart was telling his mind.

There were other hangouts, too. Another sports bar, Sneaky

Sunday, had the best burgers, if they were going to eat. They sat on the patio at Room 13. Occasionally, they went to The Globe. They enjoyed listening to live music. For that, they usually went to the Georgia Theater, or, for a change of pace, the 40 Watt Club.

Athens, in addition to being the home of the Bulldogs, is also the home of the Georgia Music Hall of Fame. It is a music hotbed. In addition to playing sports, Dan had been a drummer in high school, and a pretty good one. His dad, a rock and roll freak, loved music, and his mom played the piano and sang in the choir at St. Anne's.

In the spring of Dan's junior year in high school, May, 4, 1991, to be exact, Don and Dan had attended their first concert together. They saw Bob Dylan at McCaw Hall, on the campus of Northwestern University, in Evanston, Illinois. That night, Dan heard "Man in the Long Black Coat", "Watching the River Flow", "Simple Twist of Fate", "I'll Be Your Baby Tonight", "All Along the Watchtower", "Gotta Serve Somebody", "Answer Me", "Maggie's Farm", "Golden Vanity", "Gates of Eden", "Don't Think Twice, It's Alright", "It Ain't Me, Babe", "Folsom Prison Blues", "I'll Remember You", "Everything Is Broken", "Ballad of a Thin Man", "What Good am I?", and "Highway 61 Revisited".

Emma did not want to go with them. Before she realized what she said, out came the words, "He can't sing." No matter what, one could not make any Dylan cracks around Don.

Don immediately fired back, "He can too sing. Rock and roll is about making you feel something. *'How does it feel?* I know a lot of people who can hit the notes in church choirs all over the place, and none of them are on tour right now."

Don and Emma were both good people, but by this time, their relationship was on shaky ground. They fought rather frequently. Because certain tones of voice and assumptions of the other's motives became the norm, no simple comment seemed immune from inspiring a negative reaction in the other. Sometimes Dan wondered why they didn't just get divorced. If they were staying together for his benefit, Dan convinced himself that he would be fine. Divorce had to be better than the present reality. Dan vowed that, if he ever got married, he would not fight with his wife. To him, being right did not matter. He competed every day of his life, and he had no interest in that type of relationship with his wife. If she wanted to think she was right even if she wasn't, fine: ignore, swallow anger, drink beer, or any other possible strategy could be a viable option, but he would not get into skunk fights with his wife.

Dan didn't really "get" much of what was going on that night on stage, but becoming a Dylan fan is a slippery slope. You cannot be half-pregnant, and you cannot sort of like Bob Dylan. Over time, and it did not take too long, Dan became a Dylan junkie.

Now, it was the end of the spring of Dan's junior year in college, and his dad called him.

"How's the rehab coming?"

"I should be able to start throwing live soon. I might be able to ease into it over the summer. They say I should be able to pitch next spring."

"Dan, why don't you come up here this summer? It's probably your last summer home, ever. You need to make a little money. The school district says they've got a spot doing maintenance. I talked to Duke over in Lombard. He says you can throw some for him if you're ready."

This presented a problem. If he were in Illinois, he would not be with Anna Jean.

"I'll have to think about it, Dad."

"What's there to think about? What else are you going to do?"

"I figured I'd work out and get ready down here and work some summer camps."

"You can't make any money doing that."

His dad had a point. Dan didn't have much choice. Plenty of college sweethearts had to be apart over the summer. He wouldn't cheat. He convinced himself she wouldn't, either.

To put it mildly, Anna Jean was furious. The tension returned immediately.

"You're going all the way up there to play baseball? They don't have teams around here?"

"I'm going up there to make some money and see my parents one last time. I've been away from them for a long time."

"You don't seem to mind being away from me for long periods of time every summer," she said.

He thought, *Is this fair?*

"Please, Anna Jean, let's not argue. You can come up for a while. You've never met my parents. You can see Chicago. It won't be for that long."

"Do you think I exist to chase you around?"

Was she angry because she loved him and would miss him? Did she feel betrayed? Was she afraid she'd lose him? A big city in the north scared her, but she agreed to visit. She needed Dan, and she loved him. *Yes*, she thought to herself, *I'll go visit.*

"Dan, what's that you say—you always throw me these curve balls. All right," she said, "I'll come up and visit you."

In Barrington, Dan painted fences and cut grass for the school district during the day. He worked out at night and on weekends. One day it rained and he got out of work early.

"Hey, Dylan, how about a game of cribbage?" he asked.

"Yeah, that'd be fun. Sure," Dylan said.

A gym rat like his father, Dylan worked camps all summer. He revered his older brother. Dylan stalled out at his dad's height of six feet and could not throw a baseball ninety-four miles per hour (not that Dan could anymore, either). He planned to enroll at Division III Elmhurst College in the fall to play basketball. In many ways, Dylan enjoyed a simpler life than Dan.

That started a tradition of cards on rainy days. Gradually, they spent more and more time together, shooting baskets, stopping out for pizza after his summer league basketball games, and renting movies to fill up the empty time.

Since the spring, Dan had been progressing from playing catch, to throwing long, to throwing to a catcher off a flat surface, and finally could begin throwing off a mound to a catcher. By mid-June, he received clearance from Dr. Chandler to pitch. Dan threw some mop-up innings and a few innings against weaker teams for the Lombard Orioles of the Chicago Suburban League and the Wisconsin State League. His simply tried to establish his mechanics and regain his control. If all went well, the velocity would return gradually. In reality, it might never come back. Dan threw twenty-five innings and finished the season with two wins and two losses and a 4.58 ERA. He was not the same Dan Mason.

Dan didn't really hang around with anybody while he was home. All of his high school buddies talked about him as if they were his best friends, but Dan had lost touch with them. Since his senior year in high school, he had played on six different baseball teams. What happens in baseball, Dan learned, is that by spending so much time at the ballpark, your teammates become your best friends—your family. Then, when it's over, everyone goes their separate ways, and all of one's friends disappear. While other people were going to reunions and parties and weddings, ballplayers missed everything to play ball, and in some cases lost touch with their families, too. If Dan wanted to talk ball, there was no one there. With regard to his other interest, Bob Dylan—not a lot of people his age were too conversant in that, either. He considered Anna Jean his girlfriend. By default, she must be his friend—maybe his only friend, but he didn't think of her in that way, that's for sure. He didn't even know if it was possible to have a girl for a "friend".

Anna Jean made the trip north to the big city. Dan picked her up at O'Hare the second week in July. This time, she ran to him and threw herself at him.

"Danny, I missed you so much."

"I missed you, too, Anna Jean."

This was certainly true. She had grown used to Dan and all of his peculiarities, and she did not like to be apart. Dan lived to feel her body next to his. He did not want to be apart from her anymore.

They arrived back at the house where Emma and Dylan eagerly awaited her arrival. They had seen pictures of her and both were extremely curious if she could possibly be as beautiful as she looked in the pictures. They heard the car and ran to the window. When they got out of the car and started up the driveway, Dylan turned to his mom and said, "Oh, my God, it's true. Look at her. Is she real?"

"She must be," Emma said. "Go get your dad."

Dylan ran around the back and yelled to his dad, "They're here, dad!"

Don couldn't hear a word. The mower was too loud, so Dylan ran closer.

"Dad, come in, they're here. Dad, she's gorgeous."

"Thou shalt not covet thy brother's girlfriend, young man. But, let's go in and check her out anyway!" He said through his laugh. "Come on, let's go in."

They all smiled and said their "hello's", but the two of them did not stay long. Dan made plans to meet some people at the Kelsey Road House. He could not let the opportunity pass to prove to everyone that the picture in his wallet actually existed.

The next day, Dan and Anna Jean took the train to the Ogilvie Transportation Center in Chicago. Dan wanted to take her to a Cubs game, but, fearing a negative reaction, did not suggest that. They walked around downtown and visited Marshall Field's, hung out at Timothy O'Toole's for a while, and finally headed over to Gino's East for some Chicago-style pizza.

"So what do you think of 'real' pizza?" Dan asked Anna Jean.

"It's kind of weird, eating it with a knife and fork."

"You gotta admit, it's good, though."

"Well, there's a lot of crust. The sauce is on top. I know you've described it to me, but I had no idea what it would be like," Anna Jean said. Then, cognizant of the disappointment in Dan's face, she continued, "But it's not that I don't like it. I do. It's very good. It's just so different."

Their entire visit, she clung tightly to Dan—her man. Dan knew his way around Chicago, and, in reality, the big city frightened her immensely. They took the train back to Barrington.

After a couple days, Emma eased into the difficult topics, the first and foremost being religion.

"So, do you go to church?" she asked Anna Jean.

"When I'm home, I go to the First United Methodist Church with my mom."

"Oh, I see," Emma said.

"Knock it off, Mom," Dan said. "She's our guest."

"I'm just trying to get to know her better."

"Did you like it when Dad's mom did that stuff to you? You say you didn't," Dan said.

"It's okay, Dan. I don't mind," Anna Jean said.

The remainder of the grilling process excluded religion, but included babies, the extent to which she liked Chicago, here views of the South, her major, and many details about Dan. Then, Emma asked if Anna Jean had any brothers or sisters. Dan decided he had had enough.

"Mom, stop it," Dan yelled. "Anna Jean, let's go."

They ripped out of the house and headed for the newly opened Barrington Brewery. When it is Mom against girlfriend or wife, some men react differently. For some, it's Mom all the way, and the girlfriend/wife is marginalized. For others, and Dan fell into this camp, they simply would not accept interference from their Mom.

As they left the house in a huff, Don walked in with Dylan. They just finished basketball camp, and Don planned to put some steaks on the grill and sit on the patio that night.

"What the hell happened?" Don said.

No response.

"Let me guess. She's not Catholic?"

Colonial Georgia initially prohibited four things: rum, lawyers, slaves, and Catholics. None of the prohibitions lasted long, but if Emma had known that they had ever existed at all, Dan may have found it necessary to pursue other college alternatives.

The Barrington community may have perceived the Masons as the idyllic family, but there is no such thing. Since about the time Dan turned thirteen, he and his mom had not gotten along well. He felt he could never please her (or his dad, either, for that matter). Dan, the oldest son, had taken all he was going to take from the person he perceived as a control freak.

"You didn't have to do that to impress me, Dan."

It couldn't be. Was Anna Jean actually siding with his mom?

"I didn't do that to impress you. Just about everything I've done since I've met you has been to impress you. But not that. That was *not* a show. She makes me so angry."

"You never told me that you and your mother fight a lot," Anna Jean said. "You talk about your dad sometimes, but that's it."

"Well, maybe that should have been a clue," Dan said.

"That wasn't very nice."

"You're right, it wasn't, and I'm sorry. I'm exhausted. Can we please talk about something else?"

They did not talk about Dan's mother anymore. Rather, they focused on matters of their world together the rest of the night: matters over which lovers feel they have control. Dan had to take Anna Jean back to the airport the next day. When the call came to board, Dan kissed her goodbye.

"I love you."

"You don't say that very much, Dan."

"I'm not very good at it, I guess."

"I love you, too."

Dan had always found it difficult to express himself. His intense feelings for Anna Jean magnified this character flaw. He had not observed much warmth between his parents over the years, and he had not felt much warmth from his mother. Quite simply, he didn't know how to handle these intimate exchanges. He knew how he felt inside—incredible and indescribable love for Anna Jean—but he had no idea how to express it.

So they stood there, strangers in love, neither really knowing how the other thought or felt.

Anna Jean thought about her visit and that final exchange on her plane ride back. Anna Jean liked things simple. She loved Dan, but he was complex. There were infinite layers to Dan. She hadn't known him long enough to grasp them all. He was so brutally honest, that he said things that others wouldn't say, and she didn't know how to take them sometimes. She didn't understand baseball, but she felt that nothing else mattered to Dan, and she couldn't quite figure out where she fit. She met him when his life was at its zenith, and, in a matter of months, it had taken a one hundred eighty-degree turn. She loved him and saw things in him she had never seen in anyone before, yet these were trying circumstances under which to try to build a relationship. Even though she had known him for a very short time, she could no longer imagine a life without him.

Her final thought before landing at Hartsfield Airport in Atlanta was that before she met Dan, she had never flown, and now, she had flown twice in less than a year. She thought, *My life went from a Sunday stroll to warp drive in a year!* She wanted him to hold her right then. She thought she would feel better if he could.

On the drive back to Barrington, Dan, too, reflected on their final exchange and her visit. Dan, now twenty-one years old, missed her already. For one thing, very little opportunity for any physical interaction presented itself during her stay, and Dan could not wait for two more weeks to pass so he could return to Georgia and feel her touch. Then, he entertained more serious thoughts. Dan had been on his own for all practical purposes for two years. In his mind, that summer at home confirmed that the time had come to break away. He saw nothing for him anymore in Barrington. *I'm ready*, he thought. *It's time to go. I am ready to be a man, and my life now is with Anna Jean.*

Two weeks later, Don, Emma, and Dylan drove Dan to the airport. About fifteen minutes into the drive, Emma asked the question.

"So, honey, are you thinking about marrying Anna Jean?"

"Dammit, Mom, how should I know?"

Of course he had been thinking about it. He would ask her sometime this fall, when the right opportunity presented itself.

"Dan, don't swear at your mother," Don said.

"Why not? You do all the time."

What could Don say? "Yes, I know. I am asking you. Please don't swear at your mother."

"Fine, sorry."

Dan and Dylan had grown tight over the summer, and Dylan tried not to cry while he watched his brother walk through the tunnel to the plane. Dan did not look back once.

On the flight back, Dan thought of his life growing up in the affluent suburb of Barrington. He was the golden boy. When his blue eyes pierced out from below the brim of his baseball cap, they dominated the landscape, and others would have to strain to notice anything else. To others, it must have seemed that Dan didn't have a care in the world, but, on the inside, he burned with a need to prove himself. For all the success he had experienced, beginning with his mom, women had baffled him his entire life. He found them most confusing. He had been in every competitive situation possible. He had been successful in nearly every endeavor he had tried. He attained good grades in challenging classes. But nothing, he thought to himself, nothing, could prepare him to deal with women.

On the drive back to Barrington, Don said, "Are you happy,

Emma? If there was ever any doubt that they were getting married, you just sealed the deal."

When it came to a test of wills, Don knew that Dan was not above doing something out of spite. What he didn't know was that Dan truly did love Anna Jean.

One time, several years later, when it became apparent that Dan and Anna Jean were having some difficulties, Dylan said to his dad, "I don't get it. I liked her. They should have been storybook. It was always storybook for Dan. I know he got hurt, but he's got a beautiful wife. Why shouldn't it be storybook? Dan could do much worse."

Don replied, "Maybe it seems that way, and certainly Dan could do much worse than Anna Jean, but it's hard, son. Very hard. It's hard no matter what. There are no winners. You and I are used to winners and losers. But with women, it's a game with different rules. Maybe without rules. There is no way to win the game of marriage, and since there isn't, you might as well endure it with someone who looks like Anna Jean. Pathetic, I know, but that's the best advice I can give you. Dylan, there is no storybook."

Dan never considered his life to be a fairy tale. To the outside observer, it may have seemed that way, but for him, there had always been too much inner turmoil to be truly at peace.

Dan and Dylan did not inherit a whole lot of wisdom about women from their dad, which made them exactly like every other man out there. No better or worse off than every other guy out there trying to find their own way, the Mason boys were largely on their own. In that regard, the playing field was level.

"I didn't expect it for me, Dad," Dylan said. "It was always that way for Dan, though. It's just as hard for me to watch it not be so as it is for him to have to endure it."

"Imagine what it's doing to your mother."

Chapter 4

I had a friend was a big baseball player
Back in high school
He could throw that speedball by you
Make you look like a fool boy . . .
Glory days well they'll pass you by
Glory days in the wink of a young girl's eye
Glory days, glory days

--Bruce Springsteen
Glory Days

When Dan arrived back in Athens, he rushed immediately to Anna Jean's. Classes would start soon, as would fall practice, but baseball represented little more than a question mark at this point, and he took great comfort in his relationship with Anna Jean.

That fall, Dan's fastball topped out around eighty-six miles per hour. He had no pain, but his velocity had not yet returned. His best pitch was his change-up. His curveball wasn't as sharp as it had been, and hitters picked it up more easily. He would have to rely on smarts and pinpoint control to get batters out. Webber tabbed him the fourth pitcher. He would start midweek games and draw some sporadic conference starts on weekends. He earned that mostly on savvy and experience. First, the coaches couldn't trust him in relief because he couldn't get loose very fast, and if he didn't have his good "stuff"—baseball talk for repertoire and effectiveness of pitches—they would risk putting him in important situations with no margin for error. As a starter, they could get him out quickly if they needed to, or, if they had the luxury, give him time to establish his pitches and find a groove. In reality, Georgia didn't have anybody better. Powell was playing in the Tigers' organization. A junior, a sophomore, and a freshman—all relatively untested—comprised the remainder of the conference rotation.

The season would come with or without Dan, but there was something he felt he needed to do, and he couldn't concentrate on anything else until he did it.

On October 9th, Bob Dylan was scheduled to play a concert at the Johnny Mercer Theater in Savannah at 8:00 p.m. Dan had first heard voices there, and he decided that should be the place he proposed to Anna Jean. Like many people, Anna Jean had seen less of her own state than many tourists, and Dan knew she had never been to Savannah. She did not particularly care for Bob Dylan but agreed to accompany Dan to the concert.

"You must have heard of some of his songs. You've heard me talk about him enough," Dan said.

"I know, but this is Georgia. We don't listen to a lot of Bob Dylan," Anna Jean said.

"Everyone listens to Bob Dylan, whether they know it or not. Everyone does his songs, and if they don't, they point to him as the one that influenced them. Bob is an eclectic mix of all Americana roots music. He's not a guy on a stool with an acoustic guitar and a harmonica. This will be a rock and roll show."

"We'll see."

"What about 'Mr. Tambourine Man'?"

No response.

"'Just Like a Woman', 'Knockin' on Heaven's Door', 'Lay, Lady, Lay', 'Blowin' in the Wind'?"

She just kept shaking her head, no.

"'Like a Rolling Stone'?"

"That one, I've heard."

"So you *have* heard Bob Dylan. That's a start."

Dan tried to be relatively nonchalant about seeing a Dylan concert with Anna Jean, but his enthusiasm was so transparent that one time she actually started to giggle out loud at him.

They spent the day in Savannah. Ghost tours have become a cottage industry in Savannah, though locals claim there is no such thing as ghosts there. However, bitten by the tourism bug, they visited the Bonaventure Cemetery, choosing that one at Dan's request because Johnny Mercer was buried there. Mercer, a noted lyricist and composer, wrote over 1,100 songs and is noted for, among other things "That Old Black Magic", "Jeepers Creepers", "When a Man Loves a Woman", "Fools Rush In", and an Academy Award for "Moon River" (with Henry Mancini).

They visited Ft. Pulaski, a national monument. Thought to be impenetrable, a key Confederate surrender occurred there in 1862. In the 1700s, Savannah was a hangout for pirates. So, Dan and Anna Jean visited the East Broad and Bay in the Pirates' House for a beer, checked out the scenery, and then took a horse-drawn carriage ride through the historic downtown area. Twenty-one of the city's original twenty-four squares were spaced throughout downtown to form one of the country's largest National Historic Landmarks. Each square was marked with fountains, statues, park benches, or banks of azaleas. *When the azaleas are in bloom, it must be a cornucopia of color*, Dan thought. They sat down on one of the benches and rested for a moment.

"It sure is beautiful here," Anna Jean said.

"I remember how much I liked it the first time I was here, but we mostly just played ball. This is even more remarkable than I realized," Dan said. "I remember reading an article once that Savannah was Georgia's first township. Apparently, Sherman thought the city was so beautiful that he actually spared it from the torch."

The legendary oaks hung with Spanish moss formed a stunning backdrop to their conversation.

"Do we need to get moving, Dan? You don't want to be late," Anna Jean said.

Dan slid toward her, brushing up against her, and put his arm around her.

"I think we have some time," Dan said. "This is pretty romantic, don't you think? You know, I'm all about this romantic stuff. I'd hate to be rushed during such a beautiful moment."

"Yes, Dan. Romantic. I've always thought that of you," she chuckled.

"Well, if we were sitting here in downtown Savannah, and I had my arm around you and asked you to marry me, that would be romantic, wouldn't it?"

"You're asking me to marry you, Dan?"

"I'd be the biggest idiot in all of Georgia not to."

"Dan, of course I'll marry you. I'd be the second biggest idiot in Georgia not to accept!"

Dan realized that she had just one-upped him, but he realized it was all in fun and laughed right along with her.

"Anna Jean, I don't have a ring. I'll have one at Christmas. I looked all around, but I didn't know what to do. I wanted you to help pick it out. I want you to like it. I don't want to take a chance that you won't like it."

"Dan, you make me feel that I'm special. I don't need a big ring to know that."

She didn't mind not getting the ring immediately, but when she got back to Athens and made her first trip home to Swainsboro and told everyone of the engagement, the only thing anyone ever said was, "Where's the ring?"

"I love you, Anna Jean."

"Why Dan, twice in three months. You're on a roll."

"I told you, I'm not very good at that. I'll try to do better."

"It's okay, Dan. I love you, too."

The scene could have been described as "storybook."

Dan had to borrow money from his father to pull this trip off, not to mention to purchase the ring. Don never told Emma he had given Dan the money for the trip. Dan promised he'd pay it back, but Don insisted otherwise. Don knew the two would be married. He wanted Dan to have one nice day to remember (Don was not aware of the weekend in Falmouth, though he could have imagined such things, had he chosen to), and a ruckus between Don and Emma would change nothing.

Dan and Anna Jean dined at The Moon River Brewing Company before the show. Dan peeked across the table at her and thought she looked happy. In the background, the restaurant played Bob Dylan songs, standard practice when performers came to town. Anna Jean did not recognize any of the songs until "Like a Rolling Stone" came on.

That night, Anna Jean heard "Drifter's Escape", "The Man in Me", "All Along the Watchtower", "What Good Am I?", "Most Likely You

Go Your Way (and I'll Go Mine)", "Silvio", "Mr. Tambourine Man", "Masters of War", "Boots of Spanish Leather", "Maggie's Farm", "License to Kill", "God Knows", "Ballad of a Thin Man", "My Back Pages", and "Rainy Day Women #12 & 35".

"I didn't understand a word he said," Anna Jean said. It would be her only Bob Dylan concert.

"Tell me the last time you went to a concert and understood the lyrics if you didn't know the song?" Dan replied.

"They didn't do 'Like a Rolling Stone'. How can Bob Dylan not do 'Like a Rolling Stone'?"

"Bob has over 400 songs, 500 maybe. He doesn't play what the audience wants him to play. He plays what he wants to play and takes his audience along with him."

"It doesn't make sense."

Dan thought of his mom's comment to his dad four years prior regarding Dylan's singing.

"It does, Anna Jean, but some never get it. Let's hope you don't end up being one of them," he replied.

Dan held out hope that he could share his love of Dylan's music with Anna Jean, but he left it there. He didn't want to have to try to explain what he meant. A person had to engage Dylan's music and derive their own enjoyment from it. The only way to appreciate it was to listen to it and immerse oneself in it, and the best way to do that, was to go to the shows. If a person was going to listen to the Backstreet Boys or some other ridiculous, commercially manufactured pop travesty, there was no amount of explaining that was going to make a difference. If a person wanted to listen to quality music, they listened to Bob Dylan, as well as some of the other truly great performers. It was as simple as that.

Dan and Anna Jean stayed at the River Street Inn. The trip was a success. Anna Jean agreed to marry him. He could breathe easy and concentrate on his senior season of baseball.

It was February 25, 1996, the sixth largest crowd in school history jammed Foley Field. Three thousand, seven hundred fifty-seven ravenous people, including Anna Jean, came to see the game against19th-ranked Georgia Tech. The Bulldogs desperately wanted to win the game. Coach Webber waffled about who to pitch. He told his staff he would call them that evening, as soon as he made up his mind. In a debatable move, Webber selected Dan to start. At 8:41 p.m. Webber decided, and at 8:42 p.m. Dan's phone rang.

"Hello."

"Dan, this is Coach. Get some sleep tonight. Your ball tomorrow."

"I was giving you until nine. Then I was going to call you and explain that I intended to pitch tomorrow."

Game on.

The sun came up. The day progressed. Dan went to the park. Going into the game, Georgia's sports information director listed the starting pitcher as To Be Announced. When Mason's name was released, every reporter crafted one option for a lead that, in one way or another, lambasted Webber for choosing to start Dan. Reporters often write a couple leads and then revise them and select one as the game sorts itself out. The press speculated that loyalty or, perhaps sympathy, clouded Webber's judgment. Any writer that gave him the benefit of the doubt at all, figured that Webber thought Dan's experience gave the Bulldogs the best shot to win. The media knew Dan wasn't close to the pitcher he used to be. If Webber had that little confidence in everybody else, then it was going to be a long season.

At 6:20 p.m., Dan walked out of the dugout and headed to the outfield, as he had done at least a hundred times. He began to stretch. At 6:30 p.m., he jogged some warning tracks. At 6:35 p.m., he began to play long toss across the outfield. When totally loose, he moved over to the bullpen and, oblivious to everything else around him, began to throw off the mound. Completely calm on the outside, Dan raged on the inside with a tenacious will to win. Considering what he had gone through and the circumstances he had endured to get to this point, this was clearly the biggest and most important start of his life.

Dan was "in the zone"—totally focused. His pre-game preparation seemed about as common place as tying one's shoes. Yet, all around him, gradually, people became crazier and crazier. Drunken students from fraternity tailgate parties started to trickle into the park. It looked like a swarm of bumblebees overtaking Foley Field, as the Georgia Tech fans filed into the stadium. Anna Jean gazed around her in disbelief.

She felt like she had that day in Chicago. Only, this time, Dan was too far away to grab hold of.

They announced the line-ups at 6:55 p.m. At 6:57 p.m., they played the National Anthem. At 6:59 p.m., Dan threw his first warm up pitch. At 7:01 p.m., a minute late, the umpire called out, "Play ball." Dan's catcher saw a steely glare in his blue eyes. He was "locked in," as they say. It was going to be interesting. Fastball, strike one, and away they went.

Over the first three innings, Dan worked in and out of trouble. His pitch count hit fifty. The scouts clocked his fastball at eighty-six to eighty-seven miles per hour in the early innings. In the top of the fourth, he walked the leadoff batter, and the Bulldogs got someone up in the bullpen. He induced a double-play ground ball off a sinking fastball, got the next guy to pop up, and, as sometimes happens to pitchers, Dan began to cruise. He retired six straight batters. His fastball gained some "pop." He struck out the last batter of the sixth inning looking with a ninety mile per hour fastball, perfectly located on the outside corner.

In the seventh, he got the lead-off batter to line out. It was the first time a Tech batter had hit the ball hard off him since the third inning. He entered the inning having thrown seventy-seven pitches. He gave up a double and then a run-scoring single, and Webber came out to the mound.

"Danny Boy," he said.

"Not funny," replied Dan. "I'm not done, and I'm not coming out."

"I needed to look in your eyes. That's all," Webber said.

Dan, who had never said boo to a coach in his life, said, "I don't care what you do to me tomorrow, just get back in there."

Dan looked down at the pitching rubber, kicked some loosed dirt away, dug into the mound with his right spike, and stomped some clay back in place the way he wanted it, waiting for his coach to return to the dugout.

Webber had given him the ball, and, godammit, he wasn't getting it back. As Webber walked to the dugout, reporters furiously typed criticism into their laptops.

Dan wanted to get a double-play ground ball and keep his pitch count down, but the next batter fouled several pitches off. Dan appeared as if he could no longer finish batters off. He looked like he was done. Finally, the hitter flied deep to left center, and there were two away.

The next batter worked the count to two balls and two strikes. Dan leered in, took the sign, and threw the pitch of his life. He snapped off a curveball from two years ago, and the batter spun himself around for strike three. *Where did that come from?*, the Yellow Jacket batter thought. Dan kind of wondered himself. The Bulldog fans were beside themselves with joy. Bedlam. Anna Jean breathed a sigh of relief. Dan got back in the dugout. He glanced at Coach Webber. Webber knew Dan all too well and accepted this tacit apology. He glanced back at Dan and thought, *Don't worry about me, just get six more outs*, and Dan understood perfectly. He couldn't find the words to communicate with Anna Jean, but in a dugout, with his coach, no words were even necessary, and they understood each other perfectly.

Dan got the last six outs without much ado, and 127 pitches after 7:01, Georgia won the ballgame 5-2. A pop-up landed in the second baseman's glove, and in an instant, the biggest game of Dan's life was a mere memory. Players ran onto the field looking for someone to hug. They piled on Dan, and someone yelled out, "No, you'll hurt his arm!" Security failed in its attempt to keep the fans off the field. Anna Jean surveyed the riot in disbelief. When Dan finally broke free from the monkey pile, he glanced over to Anna Jean's seat. Their eyes met, and he smiled. She saw that he was crying. She winced as she considered the excruciating sense of loss he must have felt when he learned of the injury and the lingering doubt he had to endure during the rehab process.

For the first time, she understood what the journey had been about for Dan. She could grasp what she failed to comprehend before: Dan was born to pitch. Only on the mound did Dan feel comfortable, in his element. He belonged on a pitcher's mound. The sense of loss he endured when he had gotten hurt must have been unbearable.

He called home to tell his parents about the game, and then he and Anna Jean went to the Nowhere Bar with the team. Dan's feet never touched the ground.

He chattered non-stop, making comments like, "Maybe this is an omen. Maybe this will be the start of something for us and things will turn around," and, "Maybe I'm on the way back. I felt pretty good from about the fourth inning on."

It was Dan's finest moment as a Bulldog, but it would also be his swansong. Circumstances would soon intervene to ensure that.

Dan finished the season with a 4-4 record and a 4.43 ERA. Georgia's fortunes did not improve. The team finished with a 24-30 mark, a lowly 8-21 in the SEC. Georgia's cumulative record over Dan's four years Georgia was 105-123, 36-75 in the SEC. It never went to a regional or finished atop the conference. Dan finished a non-distinguished college career with a won-loss record of 12 and 10. At the end of the season, six years after Georgia had won the national championship, Coach Webber, who had won exactly 500 games at Georgia, avoided the inevitable and resigned.

While Dan played out his senior season, Anna Jean planned their wedding for the last Saturday in June. Dan wanted to be involved, but not only was he busy, every time he tried, he felt out of touch. He always felt like he said or did the wrong thing, and finally, in an attempt to actually be helpful, he backed out of it. As one might imagine, that is not how Anna Jean perceived his actions. Dan did not find her to be an especially pleasant person to be around, but as Dan would soon find out, she had a lot more on her mind than the wedding.

The wedding would be at the First United Methodist Church in Swainsboro. Placemats, invitations, name tags, menu options, the photographer, the music, flower arrangements, etc., etc.—one thing that is clear throughout history: the wedding ritual and reception have absolutely nothing to do with the two people who are getting married. It is all about everything and everyone else. Anna Jean endured tremendous stress, and her grades suffered some for it. She had to drop a class. Dan's parents flew down to meet Louise. Emma cried most of the way back. Her oldest son was getting married. She had little involvement, and it would be at a Methodist Church. A person had to wonder, would there be fewer divorces if marriages had more to do with love and less to do with convention, if people could start their lives together with sheer elation instead of growing to become intolerant of the other's shortcomings before they even spent one minute together as man and wife?

Dan still hoped to play pro ball. He went undrafted in June. Prior to the draft, several scouts had been in contact with him, but Dan knew at best he'd be a late-round draft pick. Most likely, because he was a senior, he'd have to sign as a free agent, which meant little, if any, signing bonus. Occasionally, throughout the season, he showed glimpses of the pitcher he'd been, and he kept his hope alive. Conventional wisdom told everyone that it usually took an entire year to recover from major surgery. Often, pitchers did not regain their form until their second year back.

Technically, due to the injury, Dan could come back for a fifth year. He had been granted a medical redshirt his junior year. However, if he didn't sign, he would be one year older. If his arm came around, he might get drafted or have another chance to sign. However, another so-so year, and no one would take a chance. He thought, if given the chance, this time he had to take it.

The Tigers, who had always liked Dan's ability and mental make-up, offered him a contract and $500 to sign. They intended to assign him to Lakeland, Florida, their Golf Coast League rookie ball affiliate, relatively close to Georgia. Dan saw no reason why this wouldn't work. He could easily get away for the wedding. If he stuck around through the season, maybe he would be assigned to a Class A team after spring training the next year, or at least stay in extended spring training, if they thought his arm was coming back.

In fact, if Dan's arm never came around, he was the classic candidate to become an "organizational guy"—a guy who becomes a minor league pitching coach, roving pitching instructor, minor league manager, or scout. This may have been what Detroit had had in mind all along. Dan had all the makings of one of these baseball lifers. While not ideal, he knew he'd never get another shot.

For a brief second, Dan wondered if he should have signed out of high school. Maybe he could have advanced through the minor leagues and been in the big leagues at this time, maybe he have gotten hurt regardless. One would never know the answer. And, if he had signed then, he never would have met Anna Jean. The new reality was a far cry from the $14,000 he had been offered four years ago, and much farther from the $500,000 he had hoped to get last year. The big payday would never materialize, but the chance for a life in baseball still existed. Dan could think of worse ways to live out his years than a career in baseball with Anna Jean as his wife. *So what if we never get rich?*, he thought.

He hung up the phone and went to tell her the news.

"Anna Jean, Detroit offered me a free agent contract. They offered me $500 to sign, and they will assign me to Lakeland, Florida. They're obviously going to work with me on the wedding, which shouldn't be too big a deal, since it's not too far away."

Anna Jean knew this day would come, but she had done her best to pretend otherwise. Now, she had no choice but to face it. She knew she had to appear extremely empathetic and caring, as well as happy for him. Dan had waited for this his entire life. She wished she didn't feel the way she did, but she was very tired, and she just wanted baseball to be over.

"Well, Dan, that must be exciting."

"It's a chance. Most people never get one. It's not what it might have been, but it's a chance."

"Oh, Danny. It's not a lot of money for a man to make to play a boy's game," she said.

This was a mistake.

"Baseball is not a kid's game to me. It's my life," Dan said, erring equally.

What is it about men that, when their grave is being dug, compels them to grab a shovel and assist?

"Well, what would we do?" Anna Jean asked.

"Well, you have to finish some credits. I figured it wouldn't hurt to play over the summer and then make a decision after we see how the season goes. If it doesn't work out, we move on. We could stay around here, or go anywhere. I thought maybe I could get a graduate assistantship and maybe be a college coach, if I can't play. I don't think we have to decide everything right now."

"Dan, would you, saying things don't work out—which probably won't be the case, but just saying—would you make much money as a graduate assistant?"

"No, but it's a couple years. How much money do we need?"

"It's not how much money the two of us need. It's how much money the three of us need. I'm pregnant."

Dan was dumbfounded. *Pregnant? Pregnant? As in a baby? Pregnant? What in the hell? How can that be?*

"What? I thought you told me you were taking care of that."

"Dan, you know I hated the pills. I figured, a couple months, what's the difference? We'll be married at the end of June."

The first difference was that minor league ball players in his situation didn't make very much money and led a rather transient life. The second difference was that college coaches who are just starting out often have to take part-time or very low paying jobs, and have to move frequently before they can have a chance for a good job with a decent payday.

At one time, no real detectable difference existed between Brian Powell and Dan Mason. So why would Brian go on to pitch in the big leagues and Dan become a high school baseball coach at Huntley High School in Huntley, Illinois, and never throw one pitch in professional baseball? Was there a master plan out there—a script, so to speak—or was it indeed all randomness that determined their fates?

Dependable Dan hung up his spikes. But he still had Anna Jean.

Chapter 5

When we meet again
Introduced as friends
Please don't let on that you knew me when
I was hungry and it was your world.

--BobDylan
Just Like a Woman

Dan called Don and told him that Detroit had offered him $500 to sign, but that Anna Jean was expecting, and that he would turn them down. He told him he did not expect to return for his senior season of baseball at Georgia. Under the circumstances, neither option seemed workable. What he would do was unclear.

Dan needed to complete his student teaching to be certified to teach English. Anna Jean changed majors to social work and needed twelve credits to graduate— roughly a semester.

Two days later, Don called. "Dan, I got news," he said. Don was pretty well-connected in the suburbs.

"And what would that be?" Dan asked.

"Huntley High School needs a baseball coach. Their coach is retiring. One of their English teachers will be going on maternity leave second semester of next year. You could student teach first semester under her, get to know the curriculum and the kids, and, when she leaves, you could fill in as a long-term sub and be the head baseball coach. She doesn't know whether or not she's coming back, but you could get your foot in the door. There might be opportunities. Everyone is talking that the Huntley area is set to explode with new housing. I talked to Tim Anderson, the athletic director, and he'd like to set up a time to meet with you and Doug Jackson, the high school principal, after the wedding. It's a formality. It's basically a done deal. All you have to do is say yes."

"Dad, what the hell would we live on? I need a job."

"Well, I talked to your mom. Dylan'll be at school. We have room."

"You're joking, right? That would be a disaster, and you know it."

"Son, we have to make the best of things. Do you have any better ideas?"

Dan had a million things running though his head, but he did not have a better idea.

"Look, Dad, I'll talk to Anna Jean, and really, I don't know what the heck else we could do, but you know it's not that easy," Dan said.

"Dan, family is family. People can change. They can adapt, and when they have to, if it's family, if nothing else, well, you just have to suck it up and fight through."

"Dad, that's all fine, but this isn't about you and me and Mom, 'sucking it up.' This isn't just about healing old wounds and making nice. There's Anna Jean, there's a baby, and everything is very complicated right now. You always think a person can plow ahead no matter what, and Mom always thinks everything will be just fine. Does anybody ever stop to consider all the different things that come into play? I want to have a decent life with Anna Jean. I don't want it to be impossible before we even throw the first pitch."

"Dan, your injury was an accident. The pregnancy is what it is. If you have a better idea or some idea how you can turn back the clock, let me know. In the meantime, call me when you decide what you're going to do."

Dan knew it wouldn't be long and he'd be calling his dad.

Dan brought the suggestion forward.

"Dan, while I understand we're all under a lot of pressure right now, can I simply ask if you've lost your mind?"

"It's possible. That being said, how do you propose we feed the baby and pay rent? You could finish up your degree first semester, while I'm student teaching. You're due in February. If everything goes okay, maybe we could be out of there later that spring."

Anna Jean put her head in her hands and started to cry. She didn't say anything because she couldn't come up with anything to say.

"Anna Jean, do you think this is what I want? What choice do we have!?"

Truth be told, their choices at this point, for a couple of people in their early 20s on the threshold of a new life together, were rather limited. Less than a year ago, Dan determined he had to leave, but he would go home again.

The moment Dan had dreamed of since his sophomore year in high school had finally arrived. The dream became more vivid during his sophomore year in college, and now it was real.

The First United Methodist Church was not exactly packed. On Dan's side, Emma's brothers, Charlie and Robert, brought their families south, and after a lengthy debate, Emma's parents decided in favor of the trip. Don's brother and sister also found a way to bring their families' to the Peach Tree State for the festivities.

Louise, of course, was there, and her parents, and many of her friends. Grandma and Grandpa Simpson were also there, along with Eugene's four brothers and sisters and their families.

At the ceremony, Joey, an usher, managed a reasonable level of sobriety. Dan, Dylan, the best man, and Billy, the other groomsman, joined him in the parking lot for a couple of shots of whiskey just before heading into the church. It seemed like the thing to do, but they cut themselves off with that. Pretty much everyone else Dan might have considered asking to be in his wedding party or even invited to the wedding was off playing ball somewhere. Betsy and Cynthia, the maid of honor, stood up for Anna Jean.

Grandpa Simpson gave Anna Jean away. At this point, Dan shuddered. Not because of the magnitude of the moment, but rather because of the chilling thought that popped into his head. Do I love Anna Jean, or am I in love with the idea of Anna Jean? He figured it had to be love. If it wasn't, how would he know otherwise?

"I do," Dan said.

He slipped the ring on her finger.

"You may kiss the bride," the minister said.

Dan obliged.

And with that, Anna Jean Simpson became Anna Jean Mason, and Dan Mason entered manhood. Some might be inclined to suggest he became a man at the Cape. Either way, Dan learned that it did not matter. He learned that one cannot let others determine another's manhood on their behalf. He believed, based on all he knew, that each person must answer that question on his own.

Dan and Anna Jean kept so busy entertaining their guests that they didn't talk to each other much during the reception. Dan considered the evening rather anticlimactic. Other than the obligatory dances and as many slow dances as he could finagle with Anna Jean, Dan did not dance at the wedding. He was very self-conscious about dancing and imagined other people laughing at him. He thought nothing looked more ridiculous than guys dancing, an opinion which others reinforced repeatedly throughout the evening. One time, though, he couldn't help but chuckle at Billy, who, two weeks prior to the wedding, had broken up with his girlfriend and, at the end of the night, in a drunken stupor, he spotted slow dancing with a chair.

Other locals attended the reception. The McBride boys lived up to their reputation as rabble rousers and got along pretty well with Joey and his friends. However, they managed a reasonable level of decorum. Compared to most, the wedding would be considered a small affair, but after all the planning, hoopla, tears, and unusual circumstances and complications, smiles dominated the evening and happiness filled the hall.

Then, after a short, tightly-budgeted stay in Savannah to recapture some of the aura of their official promise to each other, they headed north of the Mason-Dixon line to Barrington, where Don Mason was a legend, Dan Mason would need to meet with Tim Anderson and Doug Jackson just to try to secure something that might or might not lead to a permanent paycheck, and Anna Jean Mason-nee-Simpson was expecting to become a mother.

Chapter 6

There's too much confusion, I can't get no relief.

--Bob Dylan
All Along the Watchtower

Dan and Anna Jean decided to take both of their vehicles to Illinois rather than try to sell one. Dan rented a small trailer and pulled his Chevy Corsica behind him, and Anna Jean followed him north in her Honda Civic. Prior to the wedding, they had brought all of their personal possessions fit to make the journey to Louise's house. They left Savannah, swung through Swainsboro, and stayed the night at Louise's. Then, early the next morning, mom and daughter exchanged tears for about ten or fifteen minutes, as Dan watched from the trailer, and shortly thereafter, they were off to Louisville, where they stayed overnight to break up the trip.

Anna Jean, leaving her home state for what seemed like a foreign land, got in her vehicle, and, despite being married just four nights prior, was overcome with what was becoming an all too regular emotion—she felt alone and frightened.

Dan, too, in the solitude of his vehicle, kept company by his cassette tapes, had an interesting, though less-intimidating thought. In *The Great Gatsby*, frequently considered the greatest American novel, and clearly Dan's favorite, Gatsby goes east to find his dream: Daisy. This act is contrary to the American myth of going west, where the country was new and fresh. Instead, Gatsby essentially goes back in time. Dan went south to find his Daisy, and now headed back up north, essentially back in time. Things didn't work out too well for Gatsby. He couldn't recreate the past, nor could he capture Daisy's affections.

All he managed to do was make a terrible mess of everyone's lives—the ultimate morality tale of the consequences of selfishness.

It was the second time in four days that unsettling thoughts had popped into Dan's head. The first occurred at the wedding when he confronted the genuineness of his love for Anna Jean. He attributed both of these panic attacks to typical newlywed jitters. The next thought that popped into his head, the notion that Anna Jean might be experiencing similar emotions, scared him the most.

So much had happened so fast, that their minds were swirling in confusion. Some people took trips, honeymoons to Hawaii, whatever. They had had two nights in Savannah, one in Swainsboro, one in Louisville, and soon would arrive at the ultimate exotic locale of Barrington.

Image after image of the Georgia Tech game, the Detroit offer, the moment that Anna Jean had told him she was pregnant, and the wedding, among others, ran through Dan's mind. For Anna Jean, it was the planning of the wedding, becoming pregnant, the wedding itself, leaving home, saying goodbye to her mother . . . It was all one big blur for both of them.

They pulled over at the designated exit in Louisville.

"Well, here we are: the fanciest Super 8 in Kentucky," Dan said, hoping to lighten the tension. "It looks as if McDonald's is our best option. Is the baby up for a Big Mac or boring old cheeseburger?" Dan smiled, hoping she would.

She mustered a reasonable facsimile of a smile, but Dan sensed she was humoring him.

Dan did have a Big Mac. She ordered only fries. They sat down at a booth.

"Well, what time do you think we need to leave tomorrow morning?" Anna Jean asked.

"Oh, we're in no hurry. Nine, ten o'clock," Dan replied.

"Well, I think I'm going to call my mom on that pay phone over there. I'll be back soon," she said.

Anna Jean needed to talk to Louise. Dan understood that. He also understood why she should be so scared, and felt his share of apprehension about the future. Still, all things considered, he thought they should be happy and felt terribly troubled by the general feeling of malaise that currently suffocated them.

"Hello?" Louise answered.

"Mom, hi, it's me."

"Oh, how is it? Was the drive okay? Are you in Louisville now?"

"Oh, sure. Everything's fine. The ride was nice. No problems."

And on they went, not really talking about anything.

Dan and Anna Jean checked into the hotel. Soon thereafter, Dan called his dad collect.

"Hey, Dad, we're here."

"So, what time you expect to be in tomorrow?" his dad asked.

"Oh, maybe two, three o'clock, depending on traffic and what time we get rolling."

"I'll make sure your mom knows. Dan, your mom is very much looking forward to seeing both of you. It will be okay."

"It always is, right?"

The next day, July 2nd, they arrived in Barrington, 931.4 miles and fourteen hours and thirty-nine minutes travel time away from Louise and childhood memories of the Pine Tree Festival, nearly as far from the University of Georgia, the classroom where Dan had heard voices, and Foley Field, where he had beaten Georgia Tech, and a little farther away from the oaks and azaleas of Savannah, where Dan had seen Bob Dylan with Anna Jean, and where she had accepted his proposal.

On July 4th, Don planned to cook steaks on the grill on his patio for his oldest son and his oldest son's stunning new bride—an opportunity that had eluded him just one summer and seemingly an entire lifetime ago.

The following day, Dan and Anna Jean, especially, were mentally, emotionally, and physically exhausted. They slummed around pretty much all day. The day of the cookout differed radically.

Dan felt relaxed: at ease for the first time in what seemed like ages. The psychological comfort of the familiarity of his hometown worked wonders on him. Though in his mind, things were far from perfect growing up, and his relationships were less than ideal, home was home. The smell in the air of summer in northern Illinois, the fireflies in the evening—every sensation evoked the same emotional reaction—

comfort. This visit in no way resembled that of the previous summer, if for no other reason than he needed a place to go, and after just one day, he felt like he wanted to be there. He was twenty-two, soon to be a father, and he needed his family. He needed to see his brother.

Don's obvious good mood manifested itself throughout the day, as he laughed at his own jokes, sought out conversation, and behaved in ways Dan forgot existed but at one time were common. Don obsessed over one simple thought: *My oldest son is home!* On this day that thought was more than enough to get him through. The ritual of sitting around the cooler, smelling the smoke of the grill, and listening to music was entrenched on the Mason patio and the butt of many a neighbor's joke over the years. People Dan vaguely remembered stopped by throughout the day, just to say hello.

The celebration featured an endless supply of cold bottles of Goose Island. Dan made the analogy of a trick candle: the number of bottles in the cooler should have been going down at the rate they were being consumed, yet, every time Dan opened the cooler, it was full. Good ol' Don wasn't about to run out. Not today. Dan remembered this effervescent version of Don as his "real" dad. Every day was a party, and everybody was happy. He remembered how, as child of only seven or eight years old, he and his dad had listened to *Animal Stories* together on WLS Radio before they had gone off to school. Larry Lujack (Uncle Lar') and Tommy Edwards (Little Snot-nose Tommy) had this gig where they would read ridiculous stories about animals, supposedly true, that their "national correspondents" sent in. Larry would try to deadpan the delivery, and Tommy would hysterically crack up, banging garbage cans and the like, making astute statements toward the end of the story such as, "Cat gonna be okay, Uncle Lar'?" *What in God's name had happened to his dad?* Dan still had all three of the *Animal Stories* albums tucked away in a box.

Dan found Emma to be especially gracious that day and throughout their stay. He speculated that she liked the idea of having control or influence, or at least involvement, that she enjoyed feeling that she was helping them, or, thought that maybe she had done some reflection and introspection since the last debacle.

Regardless, Emma's demeanor had changed radically since their encounter last summer. Likewise, his dad struck him as noticeably different. Then Dan figured it out: his parents were getting along with each other splendidly. They hadn't raised their voices to each other at all since he and Anna Jean had arrived. *Odd*, Dan thought. One would think this to be a very stressful time for them. A very young, unemployed, expectant couple invaded their home, yet, his parents acted as if nothing unusual was happening. Dan almost heard the voice of his dad saying, *Hey, come on over, stay a while!* Dan didn't know it, but since Dylan had left for college his parents typically behaved in this fashion. The very absence of children in the house had reduced the stress so significantly that Don and Emma had gradually forgotten why they hated each other and had begun to remember why they loved each other.

Anna Jean made two pecan pies. The pie tasted so good, it was almost indigestible, sticking to everyone's ribs as they ate it—did any of the pieces of pie that day even reach their ultimate destinations? She seemed to have come to grips with the inevitable. Nothing she could do could change anything. Far from resigning herself to her situation, she merely adopted a practical outlook: she now lived in Barrington, and she couldn't go back even if she wanted to. Deliberating over options would be futile. Accepting this reality allowed her to take on the persona of the Anna Jean Dan had fallen in love with his junior year in college, the year he had been hurt. She was very kind and loving toward Dan throughout the day, and he was not shy about returning the favor.

Dylan brought his new girlfriend, Lisa, over to the house. An effervescent, energetic, funny, kind, and authentic young woman, Dan considered her and Dylan a storybook couple.

Anna Jean and Dan experienced a sensation they had not known for some time—that day, at least, they were all family.

Don announced, "The steaks are ready!"

A famished Dan, eager for the steaks to be served, devoured his rib-eye.

"Perfection, Dad!"

"Hungry, there, Dan?"

Maybe this could work after all.

The following Monday, Dan met with Tim and Doug. The meeting went well. Dan would student-teach and coach baseball. If things went as expected, he would be named the long-term sub the next semester, and depending on whether or not his supervising teacher decided to return from her pregnancy leave, the potential existed for him to slide into the vacant position. Things were temporarily looking up.

Then, that Thursday, around 10:30 p.m., Anna Jean started to bleed. Dan sped her to the emergency room at Good Shepherd Hospital. She lost the baby.

The doctor explained that if something was wrong with the fetus, nature often intervened.

"Dan," the doctor said, "Maybe it wasn't meant to be."

Apparently, women frequently miscarried during their first pregnancy, a fact that every couple most likely considered fine so long as it happened to somebody else.

Questions ran through Dan's head faster than he could contemplate any answers to them. *Was the move too stressful? Did she strain herself? Was the blob of tissue being rinsed down the sink going to be a boy? Would it have been the son of his that might one day actually throw a pitch in professional baseball? Did God know this tissue? Was this tissue saved? Or was it all random coincidence?*

Anna Jean called her mom and continued to cry long after she hung up the phone.

Emma was on duty that evening. Due to a shortage of nurses, she occasionally had to work nights. She came rushing over. Dan looked up at his mother's face when she walked into the room. Upon doing so, he realized that, for the first time in a long time, his mother did not look like she thought she had all the answers. The nun-face was gone. From that moment on, Dan saw only Emma, the nurse. Emma approached the bed and took Anna Jean's hand.

Dan started work at Huntley, but Anna Jean did not enroll in school.

Anna Jean wanted a place of her own, so she took a job as a receptionist at a medical office to begin saving money.

"Anna Jean, I want our own place, too, but don't you think you'll regret this?"

"We need the money."

"Don't you want to get your degree?"

"I don't see what good that does us right now."

Dan tended to think long-term and valued dreams. His parents raised him to assume anything was possible until proven otherwise. He assumed Anna Jean would want a college degree. He thought the intrinsic worth of a degree would be important to her, and obviously, he had grown up believing education to be the key to any future success.

Anna Jean did not see it that way. She leaned toward the practical. Right now, she needed a job to make money to get an apartment. What value, in the long term, a degree might be was immaterial. She still didn't understand what things cost in the suburbs, but she learned quickly. She never did become the first person in her family to earn a college degree.

Anna Jean needed medication for a couple of months until her depression stabilized. When her condition improved, she became obsessed with getting pregnant again. One might think that a good thing for Dan, but not so.

All the temperature-taking and marks on the calendar drove him insane. Dan thought, *Shouldn't sex be about mutual love between two people, and shouldn't children come from that?* Wasn't that healthy?

"For Christsakes, Anna Jean, this is ludicrous. All this rigmarole is probably getting in the way of you getting pregnant. It's not natural."

Then, one day, what Hawkeye on *MASH* called, "The Big Couldn't," manifested itself.

"Anna Jean, knock this shit off, or I'm never sleeping with you again, I swear."

Dan could never carry through with that threat, but at the time, he couldn't have been more serious, and Anna Jean took it to heart. Shortly thereafter, she became pregnant.

Around the holidays, Doug informed Dan that the Board approved his recommendation to name Dan a long-term sub for the second semester, and in March, Doug notified him that his cooperating teacher did not plan to return the next year. Doug indicated he planned to recommend Dan for the position. The Board approved the recommendation, and Dan had his first full-time job.

Dan and Anna Jean survived a frantic first year of marriage. In March of 1997, shortly after Dan had coached his first baseball practice and had learned he would have a job and a regular paycheck the next year, the young couple signed a lease for their first apartment. They selected a place in Lake in the Hills, just east of Randall Road and north of Algonquin Road, about halfway between Barrington and Huntley.

Right about this time, Bob Dylan finished recording *Time Out of Mind*, and shortly thereafter suffered through a near-fatal bout of pericarditis. Columbia released the album in September, and it earned three Grammy's, including album of the year. It was Dylan's first studio album since 1993's *World Gone Wrong*, and his first album of original material since 1990's *Under the Red Sky*. It was produced by Danial Lanois, who produced 1989's *Oh Mercy*, arguably Dylan's strongest work of the Eighties. *Time Out of Mind* began a string of four albums over the next twelve years that were among Dylan's finest. It spurred a resurgence in his career, and added new life to already strong live performances. *Time Out of Mind*, though outstanding, also suffered from over-production in many people's minds. Dan found live versions of many of those songs and alternate versions that appeared on later records to be much more impressive than the versions included on the record. The masterpiece "Mississippi", perhaps Dylan's best song since "Tangled up in Blue" was left off the album entirely and eventually included on 2001's *Love and Theft*.

The second day of living in his new apartment with his wife of less than a year, Dan had his first newspaper ever, *The Northwest Herald* of Crystal Lake, delivered directly to his very own private residence.

Over the past several years, Dan had been reading of a crisis in the Catholic Church. Throughout the mid-Nineties, a scourge of accusations of sexual abuse by priests infected the Church. The stories described arrests and abuse, but nothing Dan read characterized the situation as he conceived of it in his mind: priests had been raping small children, primarily little boys, for years. The church coughed up millions upon millions of its ancient and infinite stores of cash to pay the families of victims. One Sunday, as Dan sat in church contemplating the world, God, and his life, he remembered all the wonderful, committed, terrific priests he had encountered while growing up and came to the only conclusion he could: there was a massive chasm between organized religion and serving the Lord, as cleric or laity. Sometimes Dan became very angry over the issue. All those years of listening to his mom expound upon her faith, all those Sundays in church, all those questions about females being priests, priests being married, The Pope talking directly to God, finally exploded in a burst of massive confusion. What the hell do all your man-made rules have to say about this? You are telling me to confess my sins to you?

Shortly before the Pontiff fell ill, Dylan sang "Knockin' on Heaven's Door", "A Hard Rain's A-Gonna Fall", and "Forever Young" for Pope John Paul II. Eight years later, Pope Benedict, even more conservative than Pope John Paul II, then Cardinal Ratzinger, who was present at the performance, labeled Dylan a false prophet. Okay, then.

Dan's first Huntley team finished the season with a 12-17 record. Huntley, a small school of under 400 students, participated in the Big Northern Conference. There were not many feeder programs or other things in place conducive to a successful program. Dan had to build all of that almost completely from scratch. However, that summer, Huntley opened a new high school, and, as his dad had forecasted, the community grew rapidly.

When Dan and Anna Jean moved to Lake in the Hills, one could drive south down Randall Road, and as they approached Algonquin Road, the only thing in sight would be an Amoco station on the southeast corner. Dan's drive west on Algonquin Road to Huntley featured nothing but farmland. Within four years, the entire Randall Road corridor morphed exclusively into strip malls, stores, and restaurants, and, simultaneously, Del Webb built several thousand houses that marched from the edge of the high school property east along Algonquin Road, daily closing the gap between the high school and Randall Road. Not to be outdone, Lake in the Hills soon metastesized into nothing but rooftops, and Anna Jean increasingly began to feel crowded. She had hoped to feel a measure of exhilaration in a life far from possible in Swainsboro, but her current situation and the way she imagined it were as incongruent as a blizzard in Georgia. Sure it could happen, but what were the odds?

However, Melinda Sue Mason dominated their thinking at that

moment in time. Born June 5, 1997, she weighed in at seven pounds, two ounces, measured 20 ¼ inches in length. The nurse referred to her as perfect, which Dan accepted carte blanche, as she was indisputably a spitting image of her mother. Couples in this exceedingly progressive generation frequently uttered the phrase "we're having a baby" to refer to childbirth. Dan thought, *"That's the silliest thing I've ever heard. There's only one person having a baby in this room, and it sure the hell isn't me!"*

A healthy baby emerged, constituting the happiest of news, but it became apparent that some women were predisposed to bear children and Anna Jean was not one of them. The pregnancy posed a relatively significant number of complications for the doctors, and all parties shared grave concerns about another miscarriage. It was an extremely difficult birth, and, all factors considered, the doctor recommended a tubal ligation, which was agreed to and performed.

If the Mason name was to be carried on to another generation, Dylan would have to be up to the task.

Chapter 7

May you build a ladder to the stars
And climb on every rung
May you stay forever young

--Bob Dylan
Forever Young

August came, and Dan had begun to prepare for his first year as a full-time teacher at Huntley. Anna Jean decided to quit her job to stay home with the baby. With the high cost of daycare, at least until Melinda Sue got older, it seemed the prudent thing to do. Anna Jean was a long way from home and did not know too many people. Though a doting, caring mother, she began to feel confined by staring at the inside of the apartment walls.

About a month into the school year, she approached Dan with a question. "Dan, what do you think about buying a house?"

"I think that's a great idea for people who have two things: enough money for a down payment and enough money to make monthly payments."

"Don't you think rent is like throwing money away? Isn't that what they say?"

"Anna Jean, a modest house around here would cost at least $170,000."

It was then that she really started to understand how expensive living in the suburbs could be.

Anna Jean had been self-conscious about her appearance since the birth of Melinda Sue, and, at least for the time being, settled for joining Curves and working out there. It got her out of the apartment and gave her something to look forward to.

Dan led an active life, but that didn't stop him from becoming a little sensitive about his appearance, too. He had gained about ten pounds since he had left the University of Georgia. Dan also decided to make it a priority to stay fit. His dad had let himself get out of shape and had gained a great deal of weight over the past couple of years. Dan currently weighed in at 225 pounds. His dad was up to 230 pounds. Dan had been worried about his dad's health for a while. So far, it had not become an issue. Dan made sure that he went in to work early a couple days a week and played basketball with some of the younger staff. He jogged regularly and remained active through his coaching. Dan figured, if he coached, he should be a decent role model and look fit. He considered it a matter of pride. In the back of his mind, he also entertained the nagging concern that his beautiful wife might lose interest in him.

Teaching exhausted Dan. He spent hours planning lessons and grading papers. In some ways, it was drudgery, but each day he turned a page on his little baseball desk calendar and read the quote of the day, and, then, finally, it read "St. Patrick's Day." Dan came home from baseball practice, went into the cupboard, and pulled down a beer pitcher. He found the Easter egg kit that Anna Jean had picked up in anticipation of their first ever foray into dying Easter eggs, and carefully plopped a few drops of blue food coloring into the pitcher. Then he poured several Old Style Lights into the pitcher until the beer was a perfect shade of green. He had learned that trick from Don.

"Want a beer, Anna Jean?"

"Sure, thanks."

She walked into the room, and Dan was taking some corned beef out of the package that he had bought along with the beer on his way home.

"You have a celebration in mind tonight, do you, Dan?"

"Why not? Fun hasn't exactly been falling on our laps lately. Why not make a little ourselves?" and he kissed her.

They had a nice evening, but, in general, the good times had been infrequent, and they would not get better anytime soon. The daily battle between the infield at Huntley High School and the settling of the frost had commenced, and, during one of his jogs, Dan even saw that some crocuses were winning their fights to see daylight. This led to the inescapable conclusion that baseball season couldn't be far away—a blessing for Dan, a curse for Anna Jean. Dan's 1998 team improved to a 15-12 season record, which in no way altered other inherent realities. The Chicago spring made each day's schedule tentative, and every change seemed to conflict with one of Anna Jean's scheduled workouts or hair appointments. One Saturday Huntley traveled to Byron, for an 11:00 a.m. double-header, for which Dan left the house at 8:15 a.m., returned exhausted around 5:00 p.m., and spent most of Sunday doing school work. The following Tuesday, Huntley headed to Johnsburg for a 4:30 p.m. game. Dan got home from that one around 8:00 p.m.

Later that spring, a rather significant development at Huntley would have an impact on Dan. Tim was named the middle school principal for the following year, which meant the athletic director position would be open. Tim, a Beatles fan, and Dan got along well, despite the inevitable Beatles vs. Bob Dylan arguments. Being still a rather small school, there were far from a plethora of internal or external candidates. Dan had never considered the idea of becoming an AD, mostly because he thought of himself as a coach. However, despite his youth, Tim approached Dan about his interest in the position and advocated on his behalf.

"What do you think I should do, Anna Jean? Should I take it?"

Knowing full well that this meant even crazier hours, Anna Jean still replied, "We need the money. What choice is there?"

One practical reality—money—framed every conversation when it came to choices in their lives, which really meant that, most of the time, they didn't actually have a choice to make. Dan accepted the position. Dan could continue coaching because, though a raise in pay, Huntley did not classify its athletic director as an administrator.

His second year in the classroom went much smoother, but the AD responsibilities ran him ragged. Dan went from having commitments in the spring and with the summer ball program to being at the school virtually every night all year. Friday night home football games were a nightmare. Dan ensured the field was set up and opened up properly, met the visiting team and the officials, babysat the communities' middle school-aged children all night, locked up, and, by the time he got home, it was usually after eleven and always with sore feet. Often, he had to get up early to get a cross country meet, volleyball tournament, or some other event going. The winter featured basketball. At least, in the fall and spring, the games started around four or four-thirty. Varsity basketball games, though much easier to supervise than football, usually started around 7:15 p.m., and between the boys and the girls' games, Dan was at the gym several times a week. By the time Dan got home, Anna Jean was often in bed (and not necessarily looking forward to his arrival), and Dan simply threw a frozen pizza in the oven, sifted through the newspapers, maybe watched an old rerun on TV, and tried to catch a little sleep before it started all over again. Rarely did they eat a meal together.

Anna Jean didn't say too much, because, really, what could she say? For his part, Dan tried to look past anything that might bother him. The way they interacted could best be described as civil.

One time that spring, something happened that particularly tested Dan's patience. He returned home one Saturday after being gone all day. His team played at Burlington, and then he hung around at the conference track meet, which Huntley had hosted, until the last pole vaulter had vaulted. When he got back, he saw Anna Jean going through his T-shirts.

"What are you doing?"

"Dan, do you really need all these? You don't wear a lot of these anymore. You must have 100 of them. We don't have any room, Dan." She seemed oddly overwhelmed by his T-shirts.

"Well, need, no. But, so what? Nobody needs half of what they have."

"Dan, they're just T-shirts. Are there any you can get rid of?"

Dan had a rather extensive T-shirt collection. They consisted of old athletic gear representing the teams he had played on, or that had the dates and places of many of the tournaments he'd pitched in, or shirts that represented some of the various areas he was fortunate enough to visit, and, of course, a wide variety of Bob T-shirts.

"Those aren't shirts, Anna Jean. Those are memories. I'll look. I'll get rid of some of them for you."

Dan had not yet fallen victim, as many athletes do, to completely living in the past. However, as he tried to make sense of his current situation, he could not yet completely let go, either.

Dan often took Melinda Sue to the park, read to her, fed her, and changed her diapers. Over the years, he would teach her to ride a bike, watch children's DVD's with her, and cry the first time she read actual words to him. He tried to be a good husband, preparing meals and helping out with the household chores when he could. He did not take his responsibilities as a husband and father lightly, but he did not know how much more he could humanly do. Increasingly, he felt that not only was nothing ever good enough, but that his wife completely overlooked his contributions in these areas entirely. She complained if she felt he wasn't doing something she thought he was supposed to be doing, and he could be going out of his way to be helpful in one way or another, and she would walk right past him, as if he wasn't even there. That feeling did not improve over the years and, in fact, got worse.

Dan tried to make more time for his wife and girl over the summer. They went to the beach in Crystal Lake, where Anna Jean caught the attention of many a wandering eye.

One day that summer, while sitting on a blanket making sand castles with Melinda Sue, Anna Jean asked, "Dan, do you plan to coach forever?"

"Well, I guess I always thought of myself as a coach. What else would I do?"

"Did you ever think about becoming an administrator? I mean, if you're going to be at the school every night, maybe you could at least get paid fairly for it."

"Well, I guess I never thought about that. If I do that, I'd have to give up coaching."

"Would that be so bad?"

"I guess, if I were an administrator, we'd get our family health insurance and retirement paid for."

By not refuting or elaborating on her question, Dan had tacitly approved of the idea, and he made arrangements to enroll in a master's program at Northern Illinois University in DeKalb to obtain the Type 75 license necessary to become an administrator in Illinois in the fall.

Soon, the city shot off fireworks at the lake, and then, before Dan knew it, the calendar said August, and summer was gone. All the fall practices began, and before anyone realized what had happened, Dan had begun his third full year at Huntley. In addition to all of his ongoing responsibilities, Dan drove to DeKalb once a week for class. Dan didn't sleep well in general, but now he often found himself too exhausted to sleep, which only those who have been there can understand. He turned the summer program over to his assistant and took three classes each of the following summers.

He completed his coursework over the summer of 2000 and had only his internship left to complete that fall.

Over those two-plus years, Anna Jean became increasingly irritable. Dan ran in every which direction, trying to do his job, position himself to someday support his family better, be a good dad, and at least fend off Anna Jean's frustrations before they blew up into some kind of major donnybrook. Dan would have accepted even a mild degree of appreciation, as compared to the scorn he was subjected to on a daily basis. Just once he wished he could hear her say, "Dan, I am proud of you."

Anna Jean could not put her finger on what was wrong, but when she agreed to marry Dan, she had envisioned an entirely different life. On the treadmill at Curves, her daily forty-five minute respite from it all, the same thought constantly came into her head. *This is too much; it's too much; it's too much.* No matter how she tried to compose herself and maintain a semblance of control, she couldn't fend it off. The thought kept popping back into her head. Every day, the same thought.

Dan always wondered what had changed his dad. At this stage in his life, Dan hypothesized two things: lack of sex and lack of money. He assumed that Anna Jean, being human, must enjoy sex, and so, as he always did, began to look within to try to ascertain what the problem might be. He figured he must just be a completely lousy lover: that he was incompetent and incapable of satisfying her. One time, when he was browsing through the magazine racks in a Walgreen's store, he looked through some of the popular women's magazines that he assumed most women, including his wife, read. He became furious. He concluded that most people were engaging in seemingly enjoyable behaviors, except him. If these things did indeed interest Anna Jean, then it must be that he did not.

Suddenly, what did not matter that weekend at the Cape—that shared magic supposedly just between them, the only two people in the world who could ever be so in love—began to matter. Dan's mind was on fire: *Who had she been with in the past? What could he do to make her happy? Why was she dissatisfied? What did he need to know that he did not know? Why didn't she love him? Why was he good enough for her then, but not now?*

It got so that Dan took to trying various supplements he had discovered on the shelves at Walgreen's and regularly did exercises he had stumbled upon on the Internet. He tried to hide the money he had spent on the supplements in such ways that he wouldn't get questioned. He thought they helped him physically (though maybe it was all psychological), but he could really never know. His experience told him that to be good at anything required adequate practice, and, without that, Dan could not ascertain if anything he did actually helped. So, he stopped purchasing the supplements and saved the money. Using them seemed like an exercise in futility anyway, considering that even if they were working, Dan couldn't exactly claim to be reaping much in the way of benefit.

Dan developed what he called, the "Assumption of No Interest Doctrine". It worked like this. If he got his hopes up, he would only end up disappointed, so he assumed nothing would happen in bed between the two of them, thinking that, if something actually did, he could feel good about it. That worked for a while, but eventually, it got so bad for him that his difficulty sleeping became more pronounced. Many nights, he lay awake, just staring at the ceiling. Sometimes, when fortunate enough to be approximately half-asleep, but asleep enough to be paralyzed to the point of not being able to move, he dreamed of Anna Jean making advances toward him. The touch and feel of her body infused so much pleasure and enjoyment into him that his mind became tricked for moments into thinking the sensation he felt was actually real. Then, he became conscious enough to realize it was a hoax. Anna Jean was not touching him. In actuality, she could be found lying several feet away from him, sound asleep.

One time, Dan rolled from this vision immediately into a dream. In the dream, he was the producer for The Talking Heads seminal concert film, *Stop Making Sense*. There were several video editors in a room and multiple TV screens with footage from the song, "Once in a Lifetime". Cameras were shooting singer David Byrne from various angles, as Dan peered at multiple screens, telling the technicians which shots to mix at different points throughout the song. "And you may find yourself in a beautiful house (*that shot there, I want that one*), with a beautiful wife (*use that camera, that the one right there*)/And you may ask yourself, well . . . how did I get here (*perfect, camera three, keep it*) . . . And you may tell yourself/that is not my beautiful house!/ And you may tell yourself/that is not my beautiful wife! (*I gotta have that shot right there, can you zoom it in?*)"—then into the chorus with the rest of the Talking Heads on backing vocals—"Letting the days go by/let the water hold me down/Letting the days go by/water flowing underground/Into the blue again/after the money's gone/Once in a lifetime/water flowing underground (*can you get him from the side here, just as he turns his head?*)—and then as Byrne does the famous karate chop on his arm—"Same as it ever was . . . same as it ever was . . . same as it ever was/Same as it ever was . . . same as it ever was . . . same as it ever was/Same as it ever was . . . same as it ever was." As Byrne hit the last one, Dan bolted upright on his side of the bed, screaming.

Anna Jean said, "Dan, are you okay? Is something wrong?"

"I'm fine. I'm fine."

Dan didn't know which lasted longer, his nights or his days. On other occasions, he would sleep for an hour or two, then wake up, and lie awake the rest of the night, rolling from side to back to side and repeating the process until about 4:00 a.m., when he would doze for just a bit, only to have to awake in an hour for work. He fell into the habit of drinking too much too often, just to try to be able to sleep an extra hour or two and not have to be lying there for that time, consternating over his wife. Of course, on the rare occasion Anna Jean did not rebuke one of his advances, or the even rarer occasion that she saw fit to approach him, what should have been a joyous occasion only exacerbated what Dan came to imagine was part of the problem—his perceived inadequacies. He would never know if Anna Jean actually harbored any of these feelings, or if, in his desperate attempt to make sense of how things had begun to fall apart, and his fear of losing his wife's love, he came to this conclusion by default. No matter which way he sliced it, his intimate relationship with his wife became a complete Catch 22. Lie awake and listen to his heart pound bruises into his ribcage, or try to forget it all and then fail to capitalize on the rare opportunities to move things in a more positive direction.

Did he have a right to be upset? Well, he always thought sex should be love between two people, and that children that came from that would be born into a good situation. If sex served solely for the purpose of procreation, and they could no longer procreate, then she must not love him anymore, if she ever had at all. This monumental blow to his entire existence, the thought that his wife—whom, despite everything, he adored—did not love him, devastated Dan. The golden boy with the blue eyes from Barrington—he of the crippled arm—had never before felt like such a loser.

One day, Anna Jean went to Curves to exercise, and Dan was reading his newspaper, drinking an Old Style Light, and watching a Cubs' game with Melinda Sue sitting contentedly on his lap. He thought maybe he would coach her softball team someday. He contemplated what advice he would give his daughter when that day arrived on which she showed serious interest in a boy. He would say, "Melinda Sue, don't ever emasculate your husband. It's just not a nice thing to do." When it came to giving advice about the opposite sex, Dan was no more insightful than his father.

The closest thing Dan had ever had to a sex talk was the time "Landslide" had come on the radio, and his dad had asked him if he'd seen Stevie Nicks dancing in her latest video.

Chapter 8

Don't it always seem to go
That you don't know what you've got till it's gone?
They paved paradise and put up a parking lot.

--Joni Mitchell
Big Yellow Taxi

Every school board has its one board member from hell, and Huntley developed a reputation for having several of that ilk, sometimes serving simultaneously. Dan referred to them as the "Loon Board." The looniest loon was a father who had moved to the area from Schaumburg and couldn't understand why the athletic programs were not stronger. Dan tried to explain, in so many words, that maybe he should have looked into some of these things before he had moved in, rather than just buying in the area because he could get "more house."

As Anna Jean talked to the people at Curves, she began to realize that people in this area referred to themselves by what subdivision they lived in. Their self-concept was very much tied up in the prices of the houses they could afford to buy. At one point, all Anna Jean wanted to do was to get out of Swainsboro. Now, she couldn't be so sure she liked what she was learning about the rest of the world, yet her appetite grew as she realized all the other things people considered normal that she did not have.

Harold Benson, the single-issue board member, had joined the Board Dan's first year as an AD. At Harold's request, Dan had put together a plan for program and facility expansion to coincide with the district's growth. Gradually, year by year, the school added programs and facilities, beginning at the freshman level. Dan instituted a plan to evaluate coaches in an effort to improve the quality of the programs.

The community no longer consisted solely of "townies." The people moving in, buying these homes, had expectations. Old Huntley battled new Huntley, or rather, Lake in the Hills for supremacy. The district boundaries included areas of Algonquin, Lake in the Hills, and Huntley, and for a while, Huntley proper was trying to hold on to everything it could as the developers mercilessly bowled it over. The dynamics became even more complicated when Del Webb built Sun City, comprised exclusively of residents over fifty-five years old, who typically did not like the idea of paying taxes and would soon constitute twenty-five percent of the population.

Huntley's population grew at a pace of about twenty-five percent per year, but mostly at the younger grades. Dan's 1999 baseball team improved slightly, finishing with a 17-11 record. That year, the school had 424 students. The following year, it grew to 522 students. Dan's team started to schedule tougher competition in preparation for changing conferences to the Fox Valley Conference. His 2000 team's overall record was 20-13, and Huntley won the conference and regional title in his last year as coach. Dan would never be a coach or an AD when Huntley did move to the bigger conference with the Crystal Lake schools, but he had been instrumental in helping the athletic programs improve to the point where they could be competitive when they made the jump: a fact that few, if any, would remember.

Those four years that Dan had coached the Huntley baseball team went by in a blur. Anna Jean, of Swainsboro, had led nothing but a frantic life since she had met Dan. In November of 1999, just prior to Dan's final year of coaching, Emma and Anna Jean talked on the phone, reviewing the ever-important Christmas name exchange lists. Anna Jean mentioned that Dan was at Grand Slam that night, giving private lessons to make a little extra money.

Emma said to her, "Oh, Anna Jean, you think you know, and you think you can do it, but you never really know what it's like being a coach's wife until you experience it for yourself."

Dan did a very competent job as the AD at Huntley, and soon, Doug, a music buff in his own right, became Dan's closest, and for all practical purpose, only friend. Every time Doug came into Dan's office, he heard the music playing.

One time, Doug said, "What song was that?"

"'Caribbean Wind'."

"I've never heard of half these songs, but every time I come in here, I like what's playing. Is that all Bob Dylan?" he asked Dan.

"Most of it."

"I listen to a lot of music. I can't believe I never heard these songs."

Dan often thought that one way to describe Bob Dylan was that he had done all the best songs that most people had never heard.

Dan and Doug had argued about the relative merits of Neil Young verses Bob Dylan. Eventually, Dan had won him over.

During Dan's first year as AD, he and Doug went to see Bob on October 25, 1998, at the United Center in Chicago. Joni Mitchell opened. That night, Doug heard "Gotta Serve Somebody", "I'll Remember You", "Cold Irons Bound", "Just Like a Woman", "Silvio", 'It Ain't Me, Babe", "Masters of War", "Don't Think Twice, It's Alright", "Tangled Up in Blue", "Make You Feel My Love", "Highway 61 Revisited", "Love Sick", "Rainy Day Women #12 & 35", "Blowin' in the Wind", "Till I Fell in Love with You", and "Forever Young". They saw a good concert.

Doug grew to love the song "Blind Willie McTell", which Dylan eventually included on *Bootleg Series Volume I-III* in 1993. He and Dan often debated the various nuances of Bob's career, albums, and concerts. It baffled them how Bob left that song, "Foot of Pride", and some others off of 1983's *Infidels*. They concluded there would have been no Bob Dylan "slump" in the Eighties if Bob hadn't made final decisions on which songs to include while producer, Mark Knopfler, left the country for Europe to tour with his band, Dire Straits. In fact, they opined that Bob might have been deified on the spot (something he probably wouldn't have liked).

Dan always hoped to prod Anna Jean to a second show, but he could never get her to agree to go. Dan and Doug attended their second concert together on July 9, 1999, at the World Music Theater, and true to form, Doug began his own descent into the downward spiral of Dylan addiction. Dylan and Paul Simon were double-billed, and the Friday night traffic on the Stevenson was brutal. They entered the gates relieved, and their relief quickly turned to elation. It was a blistering show, and Dan would never have to go to a Dylan concert by himself again until Doug retired following the 2003-2004 school year. From 2000 through 2002, they spent a great deal of time and money following Dylan and his scintillating band, featuring Charlie Sexton and Larry Campbell on guitar, around the Midwest.

Dan and Anna Jean survived by pushing their charge cards to their limits, but somehow he always scraped enough together to make the Dylan shows. Dan found it strange that Anna Jean had never said a word to him about going to see these concerts, but to suggest going to a Cubs game together, much less with someone else, would elicit wrath disguised in the statement, "Do you think we can afford it?"

Doug lived in St. Charles and had grown up in West Chicago, but his first teaching job had been in Florida, and he eventually moved there upon retirement. Once Doug had retired, Dan continued on the never-ending journey of concert-going, mostly by himself, until 2008, when he would find another person to accompany him.

During the following fall of 1999, Bob was scheduled to play a show up in Milwaukee. Doug could not go, and Anna Jean would not go, so Dan went by himself. It may not have been Dan's brightest move in some regards, but then again, things were not good between the two of them anyway, and Dan began to concern himself less with the potential backlash of decisions such as this. Bob and the boys covered Buddy Holly's "Not Fade Away", which brought down the house. Phil Lesh and Friends, Lesh having been the former bassist for The Grateful Dead, opened. Dan found some humor in watching a Deadhead dance to "Tangled up in Blue", but what he remembered most about that show was "Every Grain of Sand". Dan loved this song. It sat near the top of his list of favorites. Something about hearing that song that night, alone, stuck in his head for the rest of his years. It elicited a certain mood he would not forget, and he couldn't get the lyrics out of his head the entire drive home.

That same fall, Dan, in his second year as AD, had to suspend a junior, Tommy Benson, from the football team. Tommy, an excellent athlete but a classic spoiled brat, had committed an athletic code violation for drinking at a party. There was no way Dan could maintain his integrity if Tommy walked. Mr. Benson—the school board Mr. Benson, who owned a technology information systems company—

spared no change on attorneys, but in the end, the suspension held. Needless to say, Dan fell out of favor with Mr. Benson, a bit of a blowhard, who, though not widely respected, nonetheless had some backers in the community.

By the fall of 2000, Huntley's enrollment had reached 622 students, and Doug had convinced the Board to add a Dean's position. Since Dan only had his internship left to complete his degree, and since he had demonstrated outstanding leadership potential, the Board signed off on this recommendation. That fall, Doug had to sign off on disciplinary referrals, but beginning in the spring, Dan could legally handle all discipline and evaluate teachers.

An agitated country faced a tumultuous fall. Throughout the Nineties, the information technology industry exploded, primarily due to the Internet, and people were able to communicate instantaneously. Everyone all over the world had immediate access to the same information, and printed material became dated upon production. The newspapers that Dan read to learn about the troubled times began to struggle for relevance and viability. One could imagine the corresponding financial extravaganza. Investors lined up to purchase stock of hundreds and thousands of dot-com start-ups and auxiliary technology-related software and services. In 2000, the majority of the dot-com's simply ceased trading before they had ever made a profit. The bubble burst, again sending shock waves through the economy.

In October, a suicide bomber affiliated with the terrorist organization Al-Qaeda, headed by Osama bin Laden, attacked the USS Cole stationed in the Yemeni port of Aden. Seventeen American sailors were killed.

In November, Clinton's Vice President, Al Gore, ran for president against Dick Cheney, disguised as George Bush, the son. Gore won the popular vote, but lost the electoral vote by five votes. On election night, the television networks declared Florida for Gore, which would have given him the election. Bush disputed that assertion, and the networks retracted. Early the next morning, the networks declared Bush the winner of Florida and its twenty-five electoral votes, thus giving him the presidency. As the final vote totals continued to come in, the narrow margin of under 2,000 votes caused Gore to withdraw his concession and set off a flurry of recounts. One month later, the Supreme Court ruled 7-2 that Florida's plan for recounting the votes was unconstitutional, and, in a separate 5-4 ruling, declared that Florida must end its recount and certify the election. Kathleen Harris, the Republican Secretary of the State of Florida and co-chair of Bush's re-election campaign in Florida, obliged. The fact that Bush's brother Jeb was Governor of Florida did not do much to assuage the conspiracy theorists. The election, an Arthurian battle for the conscience of the country, had repercussions would be felt for some time.

In January, theoretically a "new" year, on his last day in office, Clinton pardoned 141 people, including his brother, Roger. The country suffered from what came to be known as Clinton Fatigue. With its new monarch in tow, the country freed itself of half of the unholy alliance known as the Clinton's.

Dan's battles with the Benson family continued in his first year as the Dean. Tommy, now a senior, had minor scrapes with teachers, some attendance problems and, in the spring of 2001, earned a suspension for getting into a fight with another student.

Huntley High School continued to grow. The 2001-2002 enrollment climbed to 750 students. On September 11, 2001, three weeks into the school year, Bob Dylan released *Love and Theft*. The album, steeped in traditional American blues and folk traditions, featured strong lyrics. Bob's crackerjack touring band poured out phenomenal live renditions of songs like "Summer Days" and "Lonesome Day Blues". People quietly suggested that the skill of this band actually surpassed that of The Band, and speculated that, after all the music Dylan had made, including the monumental songs of the mid-Sixties, he had finally figured out how to get the sound and make the music he'd been aiming for through all of his many iterations.

Something else had happened on that day. Before Bush could get a year under his belt as president, nineteen Islamic terrorists representing Al-Qaeda hijacked four planes. Two of the hijackers flew planes into the Twin Towers of the World Trade Center, the same building that had been bombed eight years earlier. The third plane flew into the Pentagon. The fourth crashed in Pennsylvania, after some courageous passengers and crew had attempted to retake control. All passengers on all planes—2,974 in all—died. Twenty-four people were never found and were presumed dead.

Many people questioned Bush's actions that day, but when he stood at the site of the wreckage and spoke to the country, most were impressed with his leadership, resolve, and sincerity. He seemed poised, and the country, for the time being, embraced its new leader. Bush, the former owner of the Texas Rangers, threw out the first pitch of the World Series at Yankee Stadium in New York, and fired the ball right down the middle of the plate. Dan and most others thought that act was symbolically important to America.

In October, the United States undertook Operation Enduring Freedom in Afghanistan, Al-Qaeda's home base. The Taliban regime, Afghanistan's oppressive, illegitimate government, had harbored the terrorists and sanctioned massive illegal drug production. The military brought to justice many of the top ranking officials in Al-Qaeda, but not bin Laden. The fact that the country supported the war did not change the fact that a Huntley boy who Dan knew who served in Operation Enduring Freedom, a football and basketball player in high school, came home without his legs.

That summer, Doug convinced the school board to elevate Dan to assistant principal: a full administrator. According to Doug's plan, Dan would still do the attendance and discipline but also have a twelve-month contract with expanded responsibilities. At the end of the meeting, the Board went into closed session, where it could legally discuss confidential matters, and Mr. Benson turned the proceedings into a farce.

"I can't believe you're recommending that Nazi for an administrative position," he said.

"Nazi! That's not the Dan Mason I know," Doug replied.

"He's got some hottie for a wife, so he thinks he can walk around here like he owns the place. I don't care for him," Benson said.

"Look, nobody works harder than Dan. You may not personally care for him, but I can't try to make sense of that. That's between you two. There's not a single reason why we should consider anybody else," Doug said.

The Board agreed. Benson's personal animosity toward Dan did not come close to swaying the Board to go against Doug's recommendation. In addition to a need for more administrative support in a growing district, Doug was implementing a transition plan. At the end of that school year, he planned to put in his two-year notice to retire.

Over the summer, Dan prepared for his fourth new job in five years. In July, Dylan got married. Dylan had graduated two years prior and now taught at Barrington and coached the freshman basketball team for Don. District 155 in Crystal Lake notoriously took care of its own, and Lisa had secured a position as a teacher at Crystal Lake South, her alma mater. Between the two of them, they were making over $85,000 a year and had put a down payment on a $205,000 house in Cary, as compared to Dan's $70,000 salary.

Dylan asked Dan to be the best man in the wedding, which, of course, cost him a fortune. He, again, did not dance any more than necessary, and this time, he secured far fewer slow dances with Anna Jean than he would have liked. To Dan, weddings were about the most depressing thing imaginable. At the head table, in the midst of feigning happiness for his brother, Dan said to himself and possibly one other, "God, if you are listening, please spare Dylan my fate." Considering that Dylan and Lisa did not start out with their backs to the wall, they at least stood a chance.

Anna Jean planned to go back to work in the fall when Melinda Sue started kindergarten. Dan, as usual spent as much time over the summer with both of the women in his life as he possibly could. Dan and Anna Jean took Melinda Sue to the County Fair in Woodstock, and Dan came home euphoric. He felt like Super-dad, throwing darts to win stuffed animals, shooting ducks to win pictures of Disney characters. They returned home with a treasure chest of pure kid joy. Melinda Sue sported a sticky face for the next forty-eight hours from all the cotton candy. The next day, when Dan asked her if she had had a nice time, all she could talk about were the goats.

"Don't you like your Little Mermaid picture?"

"Sure. Did you see how the goats came right up to me and let me pet them?"

"Of course I did. Do you like sleeping with your new stuffed puppy?"

"It's soft. Those goats ate right out of my hand, daddy."

"Yes, they did."

Dan gave up.

Later that week, Anna Jean broached a sensitive topic with Dan. She thought it best to bring it up before the teachers and students were back to school.

"Dan, now that you are an administrator, and since I am going back to work, don't you think it's time we actually buy a house?"

This actually meant, "Dan, now that you are an administrator and I am going back to work, we are going to start looking for a house."

They settled on a $195,000 home in Crystal Lake. Buying the house so excited Anny Jean, that she found a way to look past the fact that its address did not exactly coincide with the neighborhoods she heard her friends describe to her at Curves. Dan hoped that they could embark on a new, less hectic stage of their lives. He hoped for what everyone hoped for—happiness.

Dan would not pitch in the major leagues, and his coaching aspirations had been shrunk to perhaps coaching his daughter's youth teams someday. Dan had to dial his grand dreams back a bit. He and Anna Jean would now share in the great American dream of home ownership. He truly wanted his wife and daughter to be happy. Now, he would be just like everybody else. He would go to work on weekdays and cut his grass on weekends. He longed to find some meaning in his life and peace of mind for himself, and as he looked around and pondered his circumstances, he could make no better sense of things except to hope that this chapter of their lives would be the start of a fulfilling journey together. He desperately wanted to live a "normal" life.

Shortly after they moved in, the Corsica, having absorbed all those miles back and forth to DeKalb, died and was replaced with a Ford Taurus. The loans were piling up.

Chapter 9

They say, sing while you slave
I just get bored
I ain't gonna work on Maggie's farm no more

--Bob Dylan
Maggie's Farm

Dan spent the next three relatively uneventful years as the assistant principal. He had less demands on his time compared to his previous post as athletic director, but his job responsibilities still included a significant number of evening responsibilities, such as awards nights, dances, and supervision at major athletic and fine arts events. In addition, with Anna Jean back at work thirty-hours a week, again as a receptionist in the same medical office, more of the home responsibilities fell to Dan. The added stress of a two-parent working house negated what they had hoped would be an advantage of Dan's new job: a better home life.

Melinda Sue had morning kindergarten. The bus dropped her off at a neighbor's house, where she spent the afternoon. The doctor's office was open until 6:00 p.m. on Mondays and Wednesdays. When Anna Jean had to work late, Dan cleared his schedule to ensure he could pick up his daughter from the babysitter. Dan relished the opportunity. For the last five years, Melinda Sue and her mom had developed such a strong bond that he often felt like an intruder into their world by merely walking through the front door after work. But he dreaded it when Anna Jean got home and the Spanish Inquisition started.

It usually went something like this.

"Did you go through Melinda Sue's bag?"

"Yes, I did."

"Anything from school?"

"Not tonight."

"Did you read with her? She doesn't do as well later on."

"I know that. You tell me that every night. The reading is done."

"Did she get something to eat?"

Dan resented this line of questioning so much that, one time, he had had enough and, before he could stop himself, replied, "No, Anna Jean, I didn't feed her tonight. I didn't see why that was necessary."

"Was that really necessary, Dan?"

"Is it really necessary for you to think I'm an idiot and you're the only one who can care for your daughter?"

"Well, these things have to get done, you know?"

"I know. That's why I do them. I've always done them. You just never noticed."

"Always done them? When were you ever around to do anything?"

"I did the best I could. I never shied away from anything that I could reasonably do."

Realizing where this might be going, Anna Jean decided to back off and simply said, "Oh, you're right, I suppose. I'm just so tired when I come home."

"Oh, are you, really? . . . ahh, never mind. You want something to eat? I'll get you something."

Dan chose to let the "I suppose" go along with the rest of the commentary. He speculated that it would take a while for her to adjust well to having to spend so much more time away from Melinda Sue. She had to let go of the ego attachment of being the mother and "the one" who took care of her daughter and look at herself and their relationship differently. Perhaps she found this realization difficult, in which case her statements hadn't been intended to denigrate Dan so much as he had been the one in the way when she had uttered them.

Anna Jean usually exercised in the mornings when she didn't work, but on the days that she did, she almost always stopped at Curves in the evenings on the way home. Dan experienced more moments alone at the house than ever before, and one of these times when he had been sitting in his chair watching Sports Center, a thought occurred to him: Why not get a doctorate and become a superintendent? Dan knew he would never coach again, and now that he had resigned himself to being a career administrator, he thought that this would be a way to make some decent money—at least enough to survive in the land of Lexuses and Escalades. The challenge appealed to Dan, who had always sought out challenges. Whether it had been pitching in the major leagues or conquering Anna Jean's affections, Dan always looked for the next mountain to climb, and this seemed like it might be it. Dr. Mason—Dan thought that had a nice ring to it.

Dan did some checking and, a couple of days later, approached Anna Jean.

"Anna Jean, I've been thinking. One of the reasons I left coaching was to make a better salary. I'd like to enroll in the doctoral program at Northern Illinois. I could get the superintendent's endorsement in the process. It would be a challenge, but I can write, and now's the time to do it. If I ever become a principal, it would be pretty tough to handle all the coursework, but now I think I could do it."

Anna Jean wondered why Dan never seemed satisfied. Lately, she sensed his disappointment in their relationship, but she did not have the slightest idea why he felt that way. With Dan, there always had to be a quest of some sort. Without that, Dan struggled for fulfillment.

She remembered stories he told her of games he'd pitched well and won, yet he always seemed to dwell on the one mistake he made that might have led to some unimportant run or another. She thought of a time he had been observed by Doug during his first year of teaching. Dan thought he had planned the perfect lesson, and when he came home, he talked for some time about how well it went and how well the students responded. Doug made one suggestion in the evaluation report in which he suggested an idea that might have led to better closure for the lesson, and when Dan read it to her, he was crushed. The evaluation was glowing, but Dan fixated on the one thing he might have done just a tad bit better. She remembered the time that Dan spent the entire week between Christmas and New Year's planning a special meal for the two of them. He planned to put some filet mignons on the grill after Melinda Sue went to bed. He wanted this event to be ultra-special, and he had planned everything to a "T." He made a special salad that he knew she liked, picked out some bread that he thought she would like, and became obsessed with making sure he had the meat done exactly perfectly. Then, just as he put the steaks on the grill, Emma called, throwing off the timing of the meat. He wanted to please her so much, that he all but hung up the phone on his mother, only to rush back out to the grill to flip the meat over, discover that it had been somewhat scorched well beyond the recommended time for filets, and proceeded to spend the rest of the night in a funk. He was a perfectionist, and while it spurred him to many accomplishments, it also made interacting with him rather difficult at times. She never quite understood this drive of his, nor could she very easily predict exactly what little thing might set him off next. In this case, she knew enrolling in a doctoral program would be his next obsession, and she tried to dissuade him from that idea.

"Dan, things are pretty hectic with me working again."

"Well, when aren't they? It won't be any better next year, or the year after. It's always something," he said.

"I know, but we're finally making a little more money. Maybe we can enjoy a few more things now."

"That would be nice," Dan, who had all but given up on that idea, muttered in reply.

"Let's not add any more stress right now." Honestly, Anna Jean couldn't take any more. "Maybe next year would be a better time."

Dan didn't pursue it. Things did die down, though they didn't really get better in any measureable way.

That year, Dan and Anna Jean got a free trial offer for HBO and decided to get it. One time, he walked into the family room and saw Anna Jean watching the show *Sex and the City*.

"How long have you been watching that show?"

"Since we got HBO. We talk about it at Curves after each new episode."

"Maybe I should watch less baseball and reruns of *M*A*S*H* and *Bonanza*, and stay in this room with you," Dan said. There was a tone to the message that Anna Jean understood.

"Well, maybe you should," she said.

One day, he watched it with her.

"Are they all like this?" Dan said.

"Pretty much," she replied.

"You really like watching this shit?"

"Dan, it's just a TV show, entertainment."

"The hell it is. It has much more significance than that, if as many women as you claim are watching this bullshit."

Then Dan began to notice that sex was everywhere. Every single show, every single laugh had one thing in common: it featured cheap, base, inartistic garbage rotating around one thing and one thing only—sex. Less than two years after the magazine episode had sent him reeling, Dan went on another internal rant. Every movie, everything being consumed by the public ranged somewhere between excessively suggestive and soft porn . . . maybe. The topic disturbed him to the point that he began to notice that even shows he used to like: shows that had outstanding characters, writing, and in-depth story lines; shows that featured sophisticated humor, contained so many sexual references, he could no longer enjoy them. Some people might enjoy that, but for Dan, some things just didn't seem funny anymore.

Dan could not understand how showing someone drinking a beer could be increasingly considered taboo, but society could deem this stuff acceptable. He thought the kids' shows on Nickelodeon and similar channels to be equally pathetic. The networks can show this material to the emerging "tween" market? They can do this, as well as portray every single father and male character on TV as one big oaf? How is that right? Dan noticed that even programs that weren't quite so over-the-top exhibited an obvious lack of adult characters, or, at least responsible adults in authority positions. Essentially, these programs depicted children as de facto adults, perfectly capable of running around, making adult decisions, without any experienced people to consult for guidance. It became increasingly normal for television to depict young people as adults in children's bodies. Cause and effect aside, it clearly correlated to the extent to which society seemed to be forcing children, to, in Dan's opinion, grow up way too fast. A child would likely submit, "Have you seen the decisions adults are making?", but Dan felt perplexed and did not consider this a good thing for children.

Dan recalled watching *Family Ties and The Cosby Show* on TV with his parents as a child. He also had watched re-runs of *Mary Tyler Moore, The Bob Newhart Show, and The Andy Griffith Show.* It seemed possible for families to watch TV together then. Granted, this had been well before cable had exploded, but Dan believed there had been an art to TV and movies at one time. The writers and actors had to be good and creative, eliciting imaginative powers in their audiences. Now, it was "in your face or bust." Now, Dan thought, every house has multiple TV's, and networks and cable companies intentionally create products that segment the audience into advertising chunks. People grow up in the same house, but are walled off based on demographic survey research. The producers and the audience consider themselves "sophisticated", when in reality, America had been duped.

Add to that the overwhelming number of addictive electronic gizmos, and Dan postulated that the next generation of kids would be very different from what he considered "normal." People talked vicariously to each other on MySpace and Facebook, texted each other furiously, stared at video games—many of them extremely violent—and even "talked" to strangers during the games. People more commonly texted each other from different rooms in the same house than sat down to play a board game together. Dan feared that the concept of actually talking directly to another person had become antiquated. He wondered if the concept of family still existed in some form or another, and, deep inside, he longed to feel a part of one.

Dan wondered about the world in which Melinda Sue inhabited and would grow up. He didn't understand it. It all seemed quite different than how Dan's parents raised him and what he came to consider "normal." Dan felt unsettled by this.

Every spring, Dan patiently listened to all of his co-workers tell him all about their spring break vacations. Dan and Anna Jean could never afford this ritual, and Dan wondered how all of these other teachers could. Usually, people went south or someplace warm, such as Hawaii, Florida, or Mexico. On and on they droned, misperceiving Dan's politeness for interest. One of his colleagues had gone to Ireland, a place Dan had always wanted to go, especially since his summer in the Cape. Dan and Anna Jean had to save up to fly to Georgia for Christmas every other year, and their budget could not handle much more in the way of major expenses. When they started out, Dan was adamant about paying his parents for the time they had stayed with them, and Anna Jean was intent on saving everything they could to buy a house. They incurred medical expenses related to Anna Jean's pregnancy. Huntley reimbursed Dan for a percentage of his continuing education expenses, but that, too, set them back. Anna Jean had only recently returned to work, and while things were improving, they bore the cost of daycare. For them, the pattern seemed always to be one step forward and two steps back. Dan used to love reading the Travel Section in the *Chicago Tribune*. He was fascinated and intrigued by all the mystery and beauty of the world. But lately, it had begun to sicken him.

In April of 2002, right about the time that Dan finally had finished listening to everyone recount their adventures to him, Mr. Benson returned from his vacation to the Bahamas, and won re-election for the school board. The athletic program had improved significantly, and Huntley was now in the Fox Valley Conference, competing against bigger schools and better competition. However, Benson decided to run again. He had a daughter who would be entering her junior year and played basketball. He deemed his involvement on the Board critical for continued progress.

A little later that spring, Doug made an unusual comment to Dan.

"I'm getting a lot of pressure from Benson to hire a woman named Kim Masterson for a math position. Say what you want about him, but he usually meddles in athletics and leaves the rest of it alone."

"Don't hire her if she's no good. What does the math department chair say?" Dan asked.

"Neutral."

"You going to hire her?"

"No one else stood out. She's got six of years teaching experience, but she hasn't taught for a while. That might be why she didn't interview that well. At any rate, I am thinking about giving her a shot, mostly because she's got some experience and everyone else is so young."

"Well, if you don't think there's anyone any better, than I suppose it doesn't hurt to keep Benson quiet. Why's he pushing her?"

"I don't know," Doug said.

Masterson had had a baby and left teaching to stay home with her child. She had had a second child two years later. She had been out of teaching for ten years before Doug had relented and hired her. She returned to teaching to support herself after her divorce. Education had changed a great deal since 1993, her last year in the classroom, and Doug thought her to be relatively unfamiliar with the current environment.

In 2001, George Bush signed into law one of the most sweeping pieces of federal legislation in history. The No Child Left Behind Act (NCLB) stated that, by 2014, 100% of students would meet standards.

In 1991, the federal government commissioned Sandia Laboratories of New Mexico, a scientific research organization, to investigate the state of public education. Sandia presented its findings to the U.S. Department of Education and the National Science Foundation. The results did not reveal a seriously deficient educational system in dire need of profound changes. The report directly contradicted the philosophy espoused by the first Bush administration, so the administration suppressed it. The push for educational accountability was on, reflected initially in Clinton's Goals 2000, and eventually in NCLB. Though a bi-partisan bill strongly supported by democratic Senator Edward Kennedy, NCLB became a centerpiece talking point of the current Bush administration.

Illinois elected to use the ACT as its measure of student achievement to comply with the 100% goal. The ACT is a nationally-normed test, designed to predict success in college—not proficiency in mastering state standards. By definition, 100% of the people can never pass this test because, in order to make the valid inferences that the test is designed for, there have to be scores at the extremes. If the goal of the legislation was to "prove" to the public that public education was "failing," NCLB and Illinois' method of compliance were failsafe.

That spring, without telling Anna Jean, Dan contacted Duke, whom he played for the summer after his surgery, in Lombard.

"Need an arm?"

Dan did this partly out of spite; he couldn't deny that. His good behavior didn't seem to be amounting to much. *Watch your shows*, Dan thought. He seethed inside about the issue of returning to school for his doctorate. Though partially out of self-interest, Dan had one primary motivation: to improve his family's circumstances—finally get ahead of the game a little—and, in so doing, hopefully restore a loving relationship with his wife. When this got shot down, he thought, why shouldn't I play baseball? Dan had been throwing some batting practice at school (unbeknownst to Anna Jean), and his arm felt pretty good.

When he finally told her of his plan, she said, "How old are you? Twenty-eight years old, and you still feel the need to throw a ball around?"

Dan's interest in playing baseball again went well beyond that. He wanted to be part of a team again, and he wanted his daughter to see him pitch.

Dan usually only attended the games he pitched, which didn't bother Duke. The whole thing didn't go over as badly as Dan had expected. Melinda Sue tagged along and saw her dad pitch a couple times, as did Don. Dan had some good games and some bad, but overall, considering how much time he had had off, Dan pitched pretty well.

One weekend, Lombard was scheduled to go up to Sheboygan, Wisconsin, to play an important league series. Sheboygan drew pretty well, and Duke said Dan would enjoy the trip. Sheboygan had a mini-stadium, promotions—the whole bit. Dan asked Anna Jean if she wanted to come up with him and bring Melinda Sue. He indicated that he thought it had the chance to be fun, but she declined the offer.

Dan took his own car. The plan was for him to throw the first game Saturday and then drive back. Dan, as he typically did, arrived at the park early. His stomach began to complain, and he meandered over to the concession stand to get something to eat before he had to worry about warming up.

"What do you have?"

"It's all up on the sign," said the woman working behind the counter as she pointed to the sign hanging behind her.

"What's a double brat?"

"It's two brats served on a hard roll."

"Well, as long as you already think I'm stupid, what's a hard roll?"

"You're not from around here, are you?" the woman said.

"No, I'm from Illinois. I'm with Lombard," Dan said.

"That explains it."

"These hard rolls are from City Bakery. They're hearth-baked. You can't even buy the oven they use anymore. If you've never tried one before, you really should."

Dan paid the woman for his double brat and sat down at a picnic table and ate his sandwich. The taste was exquisite. He walked back to the concession stand.

"That didn't take you long. Want another one?" the woman said.

"I can't. I'm supposed to start the first game, but I'd like to take some brats and hard rolls back with me. Where can I get some?"

Dana formally introduced herself to Dan as the general manager's wife and explained that she managed the concession stand. She proceeded to describe how Sheboygan had several local meat markets and corner bakeries and wrote down directions for him to Miesfeld's, which sold the brats he had had, and to City Bakery on a napkin.

Then, before he turned away, she added, "You know, it's not enough just to have a real Sheboygan brat and a real hard roll. You have to know how to cook and serve the brats right. You cook them over an open, low flame, not too hot, and you have to turn them frequently, east-west and north-south, so the casing doesn't split. And under no circumstances do you boil a brat, or serve them with sauerkraut, or relish, or any other bush league stuff like that. Got it?"

Dan laughed out loud at this sandlot veteran, who actually knew the correct usage of the term bush league. Dan, who loved his grill, found all this fascinating.

"You been at a ballpark a time or two, haven't you? Yeah, I got it. Thanks."

Dan got in his car and took off to Meisfeld's and then headed south on Calumet Drive to Michigan Avenue and turned left to City Bakery. He parked his car on the street and crossed over to the north side of the road and walked into the store. When he exited the store and looked up, he saw a sign—Brennan's—and a green clover on the outside of the building. It surprised him that he had missed the sign initially, but he attributed it to being rushed in a strange town. He had been so intent on finding the bakery that, somehow, he had walked right past the bar.

Duke checked everyone into the hotel and, by this time, had arrived at the park. Nobody knew Dan's whereabouts.

Dan reversed his tracks and headed back to Wildwood Baseball Park. As he turned left back onto Calumet, Dan realized he would be late. He called Duke on his cell phone to inform him, though omitted the details. Duke told him he'd switch starters, and Dan could throw the second game instead. Dan turned right on to New Jersey Avenue, and, now slated to throw the second game, had an idea. He pulled into the parking lot at right about the time the first game got underway, and immediately began to elicit support for his plan among the guys in the dugout.

Dan pitched well. Lombard swept both games, but Dan didn't drive back. Instead, he and some of the other guys went out to Brennan's after the games, and Dan did something he had never done before. He lied to Anna Jean and told her they were having some weather problems, and Duke moved his start back to Sunday.

Dan left after the first game on Sunday and drove back, but like all women, Anna Jean knew something was fishy. She chose not to push it. Dan finished the season, and even though he probably could have played for Lombard for several more years had he wanted to, he did not go back the next year.

Dan felt bad that he had lied to Anna Jean. Considering the two lies of omission—the one that he was throwing batting practice and the second that he called Duke—and the third blatant lie about the weekend made him feel very badly. He didn't think it was wrong to play baseball, but knew he shouldn't have lied. He rationalized that he did not do anything wrong. He just wanted to have some fun and knew Anna Jean would have gone ballistic if he stayed overnight. It's easier this way. I haven't hurt anyone, and if I tell the truth, it will just cause the fireworks to start. Dan regretted that part of his lie included baseball, which oddly made him feel worse. Dan felt another twinge in his conscience because he realized that part of why he wanted to play again in the first place was to piss off Anna Jean. Recently, he had acted out of character multiple times. His mom's Catholic conscience kicked in, and Dan worried that he had behaved in these ways in the past and not even realized it.

"Well, I hope you have that out of your system for good," Anna Jean said about the middle of August, just prior to the start of school, which was her tactful way of saying, "Don't even think of doing this again."

Dan finished the season with a 7-4 record and a 3.43 ERA. He wondered if he'd ever pitch for anyone again.

Chapter 10

I am hanging in the balance of the reality of man
Like every sparrow falling, like every grain of sand

--Bob Dylan
Every Grain of Sand

By August of 2002, Huntley's enrollment grew to 950 students. Dan tried desperately and unsuccessfully to learn how to be a "nobody," which, as far as he could tell, must be what Anna Jean had in mind for him.

In the spring of 2003, the Taliban had begun to weaken, but for some inexplicable reason the Bush administration elected to invade Iraq.

Dan looked up from his paper. "That goddamn son of a bitch."

"What's wrong, Dan?" Anna Jean asked.

"He did it. Bush went into Iraq. One war wasn't enough for that cowboy."

Saddam Hussein had not been cooperating with weapons inspectors, so the United States made an executive decision to eliminate weapons of mass destruction in Iraq. Americans would later come to learn that there these weapons did not exist. Some officials accused Hussein of harboring and supporting Al-Qaeda, but Al-Qaeda did not take up residence in Iraq until a vacuum of instability followed the invasion.

Bush so angered Dan, who had voted conservative his entire life, that he could barely stand looking at the papers or turning on the TV's.

"That bastard is so arrogant."

"Dan, settle down. We've been through this."

Dan often quipped in November of 2000 that America had

"elected" Edgar Bergen (Dick Cheney) as president and Charlie McCarthy (George Bush) as vice president. Even though Cheney technically assumed the role of vice president, Dan found it difficult to imagine Bush having an original thought. The only other opinion the two of them even remotely entertained came from Secretary of State Don Rumsfeld, who became the face of the arrogance inherent in this administration, a role that suited him perfectly.

Anna Jean got up to go into the kitchen, but a little while later, she heard Dan swearing again.

"Dan," she yelled, "Would you like a beer?"

"Yeah, bring me a beer. It can't hurt. Make sure there's more in there, too."

In March, the Board authorized the high school to add another administrator, and, by August of 2003, as Doug entered his final year as principal, Huntley's six-day enrollment indicated 1,200 students. *Here's to friends*, Dan thought as the school year neared its close and he considered the impending retirement of his friend: *friends—that fleeting and underappreciated commodity*.

Hiring staff to accommodate Huntley's extensive growth essentially defined Doug's tenure. However, despite a very young staff and a slew of new teachers every year, Dough cultivated a positive climate in the building, and the test scores showed an upward trend over the last several years.

Recently, Dan had become buddies with the special education department chair, Paul Wakefield, a fellow music-head. With the exception of Anna Jean, the prettiest girl Dan had ever seen, and his baseball companions, a mutual love of rock and roll was the common thread that joined Dan and the people with whom he had become friends. On March 13, 2004, Paul accompanied Doug and Dan to the last concert those two would see together. They traveled to the Eagles Club in Milwaukee, Dan's favorite venue, to see a Bob concert. That night Paul heard "The Wicked Messenger", "Tell Me That It Isn't True", "Tweedle Dee and Tweedle Dum", "Just Like a Woman", "Highway 61 Revisited", "Can't Wait", "Down Along the Cove", "It Ain't Me, Babe", "Stuck Inside of Mobile with the Memphis Blues Again", "Man in the Long Black Coat", "Moonlight", "Honest with Me", "Every Grain of

Sand", "Summer Days", "Cat's in the Well", "Like a Rolling Stone" (*Take that, Anna Jean*, Dan had thought as soon as he had heard the first chord), and "All Along the Watchtower".

Sometimes Dan felt like Elmer Gantry, converting the masses, except that Dan's motives were genuine.

When Huntley posted Doug's position, conventional wisdom pointed to Dan getting the job. The district set up a formal interview process in which they invited five outside candidates in addition to Dan for interviews. The consensus of the committee favored Dan, hands down.

At the Board meeting the following week, in closed session, Doug made staffing recommendations for the upcoming school year and recommended the dismissal of Masterson. Mr. Benson pontificated about his daughter's high regard for her. The Board believed that while Masterson might have some deficiencies, she should be given another year to demonstrate her ability to do the job.

At that same meeting, the Board approved Dan to be principal for the 2004-2005 school year. Benson raved as only he could.

"Hire Mason, and it will be a mistake."

Since it was his replacement, Doug kept quiet.

"Why do you say that, Mr. Benson?" Tim asked.

Tim, now the assistant superintendent, neared completion of his dissertation. The more tenured Board members respected him, remembering him as the football coach/ticket taker/ bus driver/ PE teacher/ AD/principal/and all-around good guy.

"Why do you want that hippie to be the principal? I walked by his office the other day, and I heard some Bob Dylan music playing."

"Mr. Benson, his hair is shorter than mine, and if you had walked by my office, you would have heard the Beatles."

Rick Stevens, the Board president, said, "Harold, do you have anything to say about the man's actual qualifications?"

"Oh, just forget it. It's a done deal. You're going to hire him, anyway. But, mark my words, it's a mistake."

Tim's endorsement was enough for the Board, and the vote was 6-1 for Dan to take over, beginning July 1.

The next day, without divulging anything inappropriate, Doug gave Dan the highlights from closed session, and Dan just rolled his eyes. *An ornery Board member—well, you have that everywhere. But Masterson?*

"Remember when you told me never to saddle future administrations with a lousy teacher?" Dan said. "Next year, 120 more kids—you just made her my problem." Indeed.

Melinda Sue turned seven, old enough to play youth softball. Dan coached her team and had a terrific time with the girls. Dan recalled how, when she was about three, he taught her how to flirt with daddy. He would say, "Melinda Sue, flirt with Daddy," and she would tilt her head to the side and give him a teasing smile.

One time, she got a hit in her game, and in the car on the way home, Dan said, "Wow, you cracked that one. You are a great hitter and the prettiest girl on the team for sure!"

Melinda Sue looked at him and gave him the old gesture, and they both laughed.

Dan noticed that, with the exception of that little game they played, Melinda Sue did not need to be taught anything. Everything came quite naturally. She developed an indisputable ability to desire everything she encountered, imagined it her right to have these things, became adept at manipulating situations to try to attain them, and seemed to consider Dan so stupid that in her mind, he lacked the capacity to realize she tried to play him for what she could at every turn. Dan learned a lot from her while she was growing up: information he could have used ten years before . *My God, they just can't help it,* Dan thought!

Other than coaching Melinda Sue's team, the summer passed without much fanfare. He and Anna Jean fixed up the house a little, but not much else went on until one afternoon in mid-August, when their phone rang, and Emma, her voice barely audible, uttered, "Dan, please come to the hospital. It's your dad—"

Dan could not specifically remember any other details of the phone call. Somewhere in there, he also heard the word, "dead."

Apparently, on a hot, humid afternoon, Don had been weeding the mulch pit around the patio while listening to a Cubs game on the radio and had suffered a heart attack. Emma had returned home from the hospital and walked around the house a bit, putting her things away and changing out of her uniform, and Don, whose car was in the driveway, was nowhere to be found. She had peeked out the sliding doors and saw him lying face down in the grass. Perhaps his precious landscaping had killed him; maybe too much disappointment had built up over the years, and he'd lost his will to fight; perhaps he had simply died when his time came up; or possibly it had been a fluke: a random event. The truth would never be known.

Thousands of former players and students came to the wake. The next morning, at the private showing for the family immediately prior to the funeral, the Masons all stood together, when suddenly, in a trance, Dan knelt at the casket. He looked at his dad for the last time. Don once had been a gregarious man with the red hue of passion visible in his cheeks. He had tolerated no small thoughts, out-dreaming his reality so as to live as large as possible within the confines of his existence. Before Dan now rested a plastic, or, perhaps rubber likeness of this man. Dan couldn't make up his mind which description more accurately depicted what lie before him. Don had spent his entire life trying to kick the world's ass, and it had taken a lot out of him, until finally the world had kicked his. Instead of the wide opening of a hardy belly laugh, Don's face featured the thin pose of a smile. This is not my dad, Dan thought. For his dad, it had been all or nothing. Don could not produce such a thing on his own volition. This manufactured likeness had a surreal effect on Dan.

The others saw Dan's lips move. They could not decide if he was talking to himself or to his dad.

"I did the best I could, Dad. I've always done the best I could. I didn't make it, but you have to know I did the best I could."

Finally, Emma had to try to get him to move. They had to go into the main room with the rest of the guests.

"Dan. Dan. Come on, Dan. It'll be okay. We need to go, Dan. Come on."

Dan had one final thought. His dad had made sacrifices he could never fully know so that he could play baseball. He had floated him money so that he could capture the heart of the woman of his dreams, taken him in when he had no place to go, helped him get his foot in the door at Huntley, and accomplished untold thousands of other things on a daily basis that dad's did—or his dad did, anyway—but

Dan never realized how much he had actually loved his dad. He had loved him from a distance as son to father. It had apparently taken death for him to love him for the unique person he had been.

Dan looked up at Emma and said nothing. Then he stood up, and they walked in to the other room, where it fell to Dan to do the eulogy. He had been secretly preparing for this for years, hoping it wouldn't be that bad when the time came, but nothing could really prepare a person for the ultimate tragedy.

Dan spoke:

"My dad was a legend in Barrington. He was also flawed, as we all are. I think he would have been the first to tell you that. We were both rock and roll heads, but one time, when I decided I knew it all (believe it or not, that did happen once), I left him a note quoting The Who that said, 'I don't need to fight/To prove I'm right/I don't need to be forgiven.' He left me a note back that said, 'Son, we all need to be forgiven.' God, please save my father. We are all flawed; my father is no different. But since we are here to celebrate his life, and since your actions are beyond our capacity to understand, please indulge me while I do my best to portray the memory of my father as I think he would want to be remembered.

"First, my dad loved his wife, which I didn't understand for a long time, but I think he did. Second, my dad loved his sons. So, considering the concept of family is a challenge and under assault in this country and all over the world, I think it is worth noting that an imperfect father and husband loved his wife and kids.

"Third, my father was dedicated to service. The writer Kurt Vonnegut often laments the demise of the concept of community. One needs to look no further than suburban Chicago to see that. My father did everything in the name of service. He coached the community's youth, and if he hadn't moved in when he did, he might not even have been able to afford to live in the community he loved.

"We have to tell a story at these things, and we have to keep it short, so I am going to tell this story, and then I am going to let everyone, especially the in-laws, go out and toast the memory of an icon."

Dan got the chuckle he hoped for. He knew it was a risky line.

"I remember my dad always felt guilty that he wasn't around for us more. He thought he was gone all the time, and either felt or was somehow made to feel he was a bad dad. I think I can speak on behalf of my brother Dylan here—my dad may have fallen short in a lot of areas, but he was a great dad—even when he thoroughly angered me. So he tried to apologize to me one time over the matter on an occasion where maybe he had one or several too many. He said, 'Son, sometimes, other people's kids needed me more than you did. During those times, I needed to be there for them.'

"My dad knew we're all in this together. God bless his soul."

And then Dan read his favorite Bible verse.

"For in Matthew 10:28-31, it reads, 'Do not fear those who kill the body but are unable to kill the soul; but rather fear Him who is able to destroy both soul and body in hell. Are not two sparrows sold for a cent? And yet not one of them will fall to the ground apart from your Father. But the very hairs of your head are all numbered. So do not fear; you are more valuable than many sparrows.' Amen."

Bob Dylan's "Every Grain of Sand" is constructed around that verse. The final line of the song on the original recording and cited in his book *Lyrics* is, "I am hanging in the balance of the reality of man/Like every sparrow falling, like every grain of sand." However, on alternate versions of the song, he substitutes the words, "perfect finished plan" for "reality of man." That is the way Dan had heard it sung live. He started to think about the song and his own words. "Reality of man" implied that we all shared the same fate and must rely on God's mercy to be saved. "Perfect finished plan" seemed to have a softer touch, reinforcing that God did indeed know us personally and have a plan for us. That seemed more comforting. Dan thought, *Sorry, Bob, I usually know where you are performing on any given night, but I've been a little preoccupied lately. So, wherever you are tonight, if you do the song, what's it going to be this time—the vinegar or the sugar?*

For the next couple of weeks, Anna Jean, perhaps recalling her own father's passing, could not have been more loving or supportive. During that time, Dan thought she must love him. She was everything he had dreamed and believed her to be. She was everything she had been during the scant good times. Dan became hopeful again.

Chapter 11

Well, the dream died up a long time ago
Don't know where it is anymore . . .
Now I'm wearing the cloak of misery
And I've tasted jilted love . . .
We're living in the shadows of a fading past
Trapped in the fires of time

--Bob Dylan
Red River Shore

Dan entered his first year as principal in the fall of 2004 on the verge of turning thirty. He earned $96,750, and Anna Jean had begun to discuss the possibility of moving into a nicer house. A couple of weeks of back-to-school nights, home football games, Homecoming, Board meetings, Parent Advisory meetings, and the like, and things between Dan and Anna Jean reverted back to normal. On one particularly bad weekend, Dan thought to himself, *Dad, you died for nothing.*

Dan regularly talked with his new buddy, Paul, the special education department chair. He occasionally muttered off-the-cuff comments to him about Anna Jean, as Paul became an outlet for Dan's frustration. Anna Jean rarely attended any school functions, so no one really knew her too well, but with Paul being the social center of the school, the fact that he knew Dan didn't have the greatest marriage meant that most people, at some level, did, too.

Dan scheduled his first semester classroom observations, worked with the new teachers, and basically tried to establish himself as a leader. Dan worked nearly as many hours as he did as the athletic director, which again resulted in him being away from home frequently.

Masterson was a disaster in the classroom. Her classroom

management skills were pathetic. She had minimal knowledge of her content. The students did not respect her, and it showed in their level of achievement. Kim was thirty-eight years old with two children, ages twelve and ten, and Dan did not look forward to what he had to do.

The teacher contract required Dan to observe Kim twice that semester. A less-than-pleasant post-conference followed his first classroom observation, and Kim left his office in tears. Dan did not enjoy playing the heavy, but he had a responsibility to the students, and he decided to recommend to the Board in March not to retain Kim. She anticipated the worst.

Dan had a pre-conference with her prior to the second observation, and she alluded to her future. Dan replied, "I will have to see some significant improvement."

The class was painful to watch. Students were not engaged in the material or on task. The lesson featured too much presentation. Examples were poorly planned, there wasn't much for an opening activity, and there was little in the way of closure. Directions were unclear, and there was a lot of wasted time during transitions between concepts. The observation report and post-conference conversation would again have to reflect all of these things.

Dan and Kim had an appointment scheduled during her prep period on a Thursday. She stated that she had some students coming to see her for extra help, and asked if it would be possible to meet at four-thirty. She had a ski club meeting after school, would take care of a few things, and then would come down to the office. Dan planned to stay late that night for a band concert, so he agreed.

At four-thirty, Kim came down to Dan's office. The secretaries had left by then. Dan heard a knock at the door, got up from behind his desk, ushered Kim in and escorted her to the table in the corner of the room. Dan left the door open a crack, moved over to the table, sat down, opened the file with his report in it and began the conference.

When the conference concluded, she once again left his office in tears.

The next morning, around ten-thirty, Dan's phone rang. It was Tim.

"Dan, can you stop by my office later?"

"Not a problem. How's one-thirty?"

"One-thirty is fine."

"What's up, do I need to prepare for anything?"

"No, just stop by."

A strange sensation came over Dan. He could read people, and he knew Tim pretty well. Dan figured something unusual must be going on, or else Tim would have been more forthcoming about why he wanted to see him. Did a parent call with a complaint? Tim would have referred that person back to him or at least informed him. Was there an issue with a faculty member? Dan had a pretty good handle on his staff. This seemed unlikely. He cogitated over a variety of other possible scenarios. Then, he thought for a second, *Is it something related to Masterson? Nah. Tim knows she's on the hot seat. There can't possibly be any reason why he'd want to talk to me about that.*

So, Dan went home that evening and slept even less well than usual.

Chapter 12

Send lawyers, guns, and money
The shit has hit the fan

--Warren Zevon
Lawyers, Guns and Money

Dan entered Tim's office, and as was their custom, started joking around.

"So, 'I wanna hold your hand.' Real deep stuff, Tim."

Tim wasn't in the mood for it that day.

"Dan, Kim Masterson is alleging that you are sexually harassing her. I have the complaint right here. She states that you offered to change a poor evaluation and recommend to the Board that she be retained if she had sex with you."

Dan's life flashed before his eyes. All he wanted was for Anna Jean to love him, and his greatest fear was that somehow, for some reason, she might not. Now, he would have to try to deny this accusation to her in the midst of their ongoing struggles. He spent most of his life striving for excellence, and as he had finally come close to turning the corner, approaching the chance to put his past behind and move forward in such a manner that his life might approximate some semblance of order, once again, a massive hurdle, in the form of a female, no less, stood in his way.

"You can't be serious. That's utter nonsense. You can't possibly believe any of that hogwash. She's a terrible teacher, and you know it. Come to think of it, she planned this the whole time, for crying out loud. She changed her appointment to four-thirty, when nobody would be around."

"Dan, of course I don't believe it, but I have to investigate it."

"So, now I have to defend a negative against this psycho woman?"

"Dan, the truth will come out."

"In the meantime, I won't be able to say anything, and she'll be slandering my name all over the place any chance she gets. How am I supposed to run the building?"

"Dan, nobody's going to take this seriously."

"Enough will wonder, Tim. Enough will wonder. People can't get enough of this kind of thing. You ever turn on the television? My God, I'll be the next Lifetime movie."

"Dan, go home, relax, enjoy your little girl and your beautiful wife, and we'll talk on Monday after I take her statement."

Dan thought, *Tim, what planet do you live on?*

Dan went home and, having no real choice, told Anna Jean, who flipped.

"You asshole. How could you?"

He thought, *Oh, you've given me plenty of reasons . . .*

"So you believe this? You believe this woman? You don't know her or anyone else at that school, and you accept her accusation on its face, period? What haven't I done to try to make this work, and you give me nothing by way of the benefit of the doubt? Just like that. Boom." He paused for a second. "You know what? I get it. This is your excuse to get out, isn't it? The break you've been looking for. Oh my God, Anna Jean, you can't possibly think so low of me."

Anna Jean could not recall Dan reacting this emotionally to anything with the exception of the news he would need surgery on his shoulder.

Anna Jean took a step back.

"I'm sorry, Dan. It's just so upsetting. I mean, how could I imagine that you'd come home, and I'd have to hear you say those words. Well, you know, things haven't been the best. For a minute, I just thought, well, maybe it's true. It's just, well, I mean, everyone will talk. How can I even go to Curves?"

How can I even go to Curves? My career is at stake, and she says, "How can I even go to Curves?"

Being extremely upset, Anna Jean did not express any of her convoluted thoughts on the matter especially well. That much was obvious. After the initial shock, she calmed down, and for the next couple days, things were actually tolerable. She's actually pretty supportive, Dan thought.

Dan got a call from Tim Sunday night.

"Dan, you are on paid administrative leave pending the outcome of the investigation. I will address the faculty tomorrow morning. It's a formality. Don't worry about it."

Sure, Tim, no problem. Won't worry a bit.

With the holidays on the horizon, the second week of November commenced. The next Board meeting was scheduled for the Tuesday before Thanksgiving.

Kim Masterson couldn't keep her mouth shut if she had broken her jaw and a doctor had wired it shut. Saturday night, she went out with her friend, Natalie Carter.

"My principal is trying to get rid of me."

"Why?" Natalie said.

"He doesn't think I do a good job."

"Oh, well that's not good at all."

"Thursday, he insinuated that maybe there was a way we could 'fix' things."

"You don't mean . . . Oh, my!" Natalie said. "What did he say?"

"Well, maybe, you know, I shouldn't say too much," Kim said. "I filed a complaint and everything."

"Well, do you think he'll get fired?"

"I'm not worried, Natalie. I've got it covered."

"What do you mean, you've got it covered? The Mason's are a big name around here," Natalie said.

"Well, I probably shouldn't say, but you know that guy I told you I've been seeing, Harry? He's on the school board."

Dan contacted the National Association of Secondary School Principals. He thought they had some type of membership benefit regarding legal counsel. He didn't know how that worked but hoped to avoid the expense of a lawyer. In the meantime, he decided he had better have an attorney present when he gave his statement that Monday afternoon.

Tuesday morning, Dan received calls from Emma and Dylan. They had seen the paper and wondered what in the world was going on. Anna Jean avoided Curves, so on top of everything else, they were locked in the house together.

On Thursday, against his better judgment, Dan called Tim.

"Tim, as a friend, what do you think is going to happen?"

"Dan, all I do is present my report. I don't make the decisions. To me, there's nothing. It's all he said, she said."

The middle of November featured the big annual Tri-I Conference in Chicago, hosted by the Illinois Association of School Boards, the Illinois Association of School Business Officials, and the Illinois Association of School Administrators. The conference was tailored for Board members, and most Boards in the state used the conference as an excuse to take their spouses on a trip to downtown Chicago, and among other things, see the Festival of Lights Parade. The Huntley Board played along. Typically, Boards go out to eat together, and though many of the members couldn't stand each other, they kept up appearances and dined at Morton's Steak House. It was a small world in education, and, all weekend long, people asked the Huntley Board members for information about the situation regarding their principal, son of the state's legendary high school basketball coach, Don Mason. Dan, unbeknownst to him, was the talk of the town that weekend.

Harold Benson couldn't keep his mouth shut any better than Kim Masterson. At dinner, after several glasses of wine, he began to spout off.

"We've finally got that son of a bitch, Mason! Soliciting sexual favors from Kim Masterson! Married to a beauty queen, and he stoops to trying to screw one of his teachers!"

"Harry, you're too loud," his wife cautioned. "Quiet down."

"Quiet down?—The bane of my existence, the guy who screwed Tommy! Ha! He's done!"

Mr. Stevens, the Board president, said, "Harry, listen to your wife and quiet down. Don't say another word about it. This is a personnel matter, and it will have to wait until closed session on Tuesday. You're violating the state law at the School Board Convention!"

District 300, a neighboring district of Huntley, happened to have reservations at a table next to them. With her back to Harold Benson, a school board member named Jessica Carter thought that, when she got home, she had better call her daughter, and ask her what she knew of the Kim Masterson situation.

"Natalie, hi, it's Mom."

"Hi, Mom, what's up?"

"Say, you know your friend, Kim?"

Natalie went cold.

"Yes, what about Kim?"

"Didn't you tell me the two of you went out last weekend?"

"Why, yes, we went to Govnor's, why do you ask?"

"She mention anything about work?"

No use delaying the inevitable. Natalie's mom could always get anything out of her. It was a skill that her mother possessed and perfected. Natalie told her everything.

"Say, Natalie, Kim ever mention anything about a wife?"

"Wife?"

Chapter 13

The circus is in town

--Bob Dylan
Desolation Row

Jessica Carter had tried to contact the superintendent, Dr. Stanley, and Mr. Stevens on Monday, but, for whatever reason, neither had returned her calls or Emails as of five-thirty Tuesday evening.

Dan stopped home between the end of school and the Board meeting. That evening, in closed session, the Board planned to discuss the Masterson report and reconvene in open session to reveal Dan's fate. Anna Jean had to leave that evening for the airport to take Melinda Sue to visit Louise for Thanksgiving. They had planned to go to Georgia for Christmas that year, but since Dan's father had so recently passed, they changed plans and agreed to stay back with Emma. Instead, Anna Jean planned a visit with Melinda Sue for Thanksgiving. Since they would not be there when Dan got back, he wanted to come home to say goodbye.

The arrangements had been made prior to the Masterson fiasco. Anna Jean asked if she should change plans. Dan thought that nothing would change what might happen, so he didn't see why they should cancel the trip. Melinda Sue spent weeks working up a healthy excitement for these visits, and honestly, Dan didn't want to have to deal with the fallout if they didn't go.

Dan got back to the house and loaded up the car for them. Anna Jean seemed a bit unsettled about the trip, the Board meeting, or both.

"Don't worry about the drive to the airport, Anna Jean. It'll go fine," he said. He tried to assure her and affectionately touched her arm near her elbow and then turned to her, grabbed her other hand, looked in her face, and said, "I love you, Anna Jean."

Things had not been going well between them for some time, but he loved her with all he had inside of him to give, and he always missed her when they were apart. Selfishly, he wished they would both be there for him this night. Dan had tried to conceal the extent of his anxiety from both of them, but in reality, fear currently consumed him.

"I love you, too, Dan."

"I didn't do it, Anna Jean."

"I know you didn't."

"Do you?"

"Yes, Dan, I do."

Anna Jean believed him. For a time, she possessed a minute element of doubt, but she did believe him. Dan never tried to overtly deny the accusations to her. He never thought it necessary, but with her leaving, he felt it imperative to say these words.

Melinda Sue came running up to them, glowing with excitement in anticipation of the trip.

"Howdy, Muffin! Daddy loves you. He's going to miss you."

"I'm going to miss you, Daddy."

"Miss you more."

"No you won't."

"Yes, I will," and then Dan picked her up, twirled her around, tossed her upside down, and tickled her ribs, as he had done hundreds of times before. Like always, she begged him to stop and then asked him to do it again.

"Well, I have to go," Dan said. "I'll call you after I get back and let you know what happens."

Anna Jean looked away.

"Okay?"

"Okay, Dan."

In anticipation of a large crowd, Dr. Stanley suggested, and the Board agreed, that they move the meeting to the auditorium at the high school. There were about 250 parents and students there. Mr. Stevens called the meeting to order. When he opened the floor to public comments, Jessica stood up and, as quickly as she could, before anyone, including the Board president, could cut her off, said, "Mr. Stevens, I am Jessica Carter, a school board member from District 300, and I have information that you need to know before you listen to all these people and allow people's reputations and integrity to be called into question at a public meeting. It is my suggestion that you hear me out in closed session before entertaining any public comments. If you don't, what I have to say, I will say publicly, and it will be a disaster for you and your district."

The buzz of the crowd and the agitation of the Board upon her statement caused Stevens to pound his gavel several times to restore order. He then called for a vote to go into closed session. While the Board could not comment publicly on the matter, most of the faculty and public knew that Dan's job was at stake. People passed on rumors and vague information amongst themselves. They knew Masterson made some type of allegation against Dan, and had to speculate on what that might be. This woman's statement fed the frenzy, and people's curiosity crested to a new high.

Mr. Stevens remarked: "I believe this situation is way too important for everyone here to dismiss Ms. Carter's statement. In order to make the best decision possible, I believe we need to hear the rest of what she has to say. I move we adjourn this portion of the meeting and go into closed session."

Another Board member seconded the motion, and with a 5-2 vote in favor, the Board went into closed session.

Jessica returned to the auditorium fifteen minutes later. Forty-five minutes after her, six board members returned to the room, and Mr. Stevens made the following statement:

"Due to new information, there will be no vote on any personnel matter tonight. Any member of the public in attendance tonight who is here because they think there will be action taken on personnel at tonight's meeting should know that there will be no discussion of any personnel matters in closed session tonight. By law, the Board is not at liberty to discuss personnel matters publicly. While this is likely very troubling to many of you, I ask that you please understand that I am bound to follow the law, and there will be no more comment on the matter from me at this time."

As inconspicuously as possible, Dr. Stanley approached Dan and told him his suspension would be dropped effective tomorrow, and he should report to his office first thing in the morning. Dan snuck out as quietly as possible, not far behind Mrs. Carter. A reporter from The *Northwest Herald* trailed him, but he managed to dodge her.

The six members of the Board who had returned from closed session to the public meeting did so with the understanding that Mr. Benson's letter of resignation from the Board of Education would be in the Board secretary's hands no later than ten o'clock sharp the next morning.

Dan had never really considered whether or not there was such a thing as angels prior to this evening, but he believed in them now.

Mr. Benson did resign from the Board. The next day, Tim questioned Kim Masterson, and she agreed to resign immediately. Dan never learned that Benson conjured up the whole thing as a way to get Dan as much as preserve Kim's job. The Board acted on her resignation at a special Board meeting the following Tuesday. At that meeting, they also accepted Benson's resignation and prepared a statement to accept applications for the vacant Board seat.

Dan never found out what became of them, and he truly didn't care. Benson would be fine because he had money. He certainly could afford to give his wife half of what he had and take Kim in and not miss a beat. Maybe his wife would decide to try to keep the marriage intact, and Benson would change his ways, but either way, Kim's situation was much less certain. She faced a potentially bleak future, perhaps even losing her kids in addition to her job. Should Benson choose to stay with her, her life might transform into one of affluence, but one could only speculate what the odds of that might be. In that scenario, Benson's daughter likely stood to lose the most.

When Dan got home that night, he went to change clothes, grab a beer, and find something to watch on television. Once settled, he planned to call Anna Jean on her cell phone to tell her the news. Near the remote control, where she knew Dan would find it, Anna Jean left a note, which said simply:

Dear Dan,

I love you, but this is all too hard. I will not be returning from Georgia with Melinda Sue.

Love always,
Anna Jean

The obvious smearing of the ink from tear stains rendered the note barely legible—a fact that in no way lessened the impact of its content on Dan.

He sat paralyzed for several minutes. He finished his beer and switched to rum and coke.

On his way to becoming blind drunk, Dan considered a range of options, from begging, to fighting for his daughter, to exploring having Anna Jean arrested for kidnapping. But to what end? It was over.

Then, a deliberate, guttural, primeval, phrase came out of his mouth that he did not consciously utter.

"Aaannnnnaaa Jeeeaaaan. YOU BITCH!!!!"

There. He had said it.

Chapter 14

You can keep my things they've come to take me home

--Peter Gabriel
Solsbury Hill

When Don Mason used to wake up with a hangover after a special occasion, he had often blamed it on eating too much chicken. Dan had eaten a lot of chicken that Tuesday night. Wednesday morning, when he woke up, he had two thoughts: *Am I dead?* and *What did the world do before lawyers, or did God create them on the seventh day and the Bible just forgot to include it?* Cha-ching, cha-ching.

Dan did not look or feel too well on his visit to Dr. Stanley's office.

"Rough night, Dan?"

"Uh, yeah, rough night."

"Dan, today is the last school day this week. I was thinking that you could come back to work fresh on Monday. What do you think?"

"Yeah, I guess that will be fine," he said.

Dan went to his mom's for Thanksgiving. Dylan, Lisa, and their one-and-a-half-year old baby, Derek, went to Lisa's parents' for the day, and Dan and Emma shared some time alone together.

The two of them talked at length that day, neither feeling obligated to have to be right and prove the other wrong. Dan could not recall another time that they actually had a conversation of this nature. *Who is this person?* Dan thought. *Had she been there all the time, and I just couldn't see her?*

Finally Dan asked, "Mom, why didn't you and Dad get along better?"

"Hmmm. Well, that's not a question I was expecting.

"Dan, your father was the most charismatic and decent young man I had ever seen. This is what I think happened, but only he knows. Did you ever try to talk to him? You know what I mean . . ." Her thoughts trailed off, then she continued.

"He was a dreamer, and he wanted to be a college basketball coach. He was so good; he could out-coach anybody, but he never played in college, and so he wasn't in the pipeline for jobs. When we were younger, he worked camps in the summer, trying to get his name out there and latch on somewhere, but it got expensive to support all the activities you and your brother were involved in, and eventually, he realized it was never going to happen. The stress of trying to make everything work and the disappointment of resigning himself to being a high school coach for the rest of his life got to him, I think.

"I think he blamed me some, at least a little, which may or may not have been fair. He started drinking more than he should've, and this got me really angry. I witnessed my dad and my brothers' drinking for too long. I didn't want that in my house.

"Sometimes things just get to a certain point, and there's no way to fix it anymore.

"You guys just revered your dad, and I don't blame you. It's just the way it was, Dan. Not everything has an answer."

Dan asked, "Why did you guys stay together, Mom? I mean, I just thought it was getting to be too much. I expected it, eventually."

"Danny, I loved your father. No matter what, I loved him. I had faith." After a brief pause, she continued, "If we had split up, would we be sitting here talking right now?"

"Probably not."

"Well, then I think I did the right thing."

Dan had no clue as to what he might do next. He wanted to run away. He thought about Ireland, but he wouldn't go there. He associated that with Boston, and he associated Boston with the Cape, and he associated the Cape with Anna Jean. However, the last two days he had grown weary of thinking about what he hadn't been able to do or might not ever be able to do. He preferred to consider what he *could* do. He just had no idea what that might be.

Dan didn't think he could be effective as a principal in that building. He had been exonerated, but that wouldn't be enough for some. The rumors would follow him around, and he would always be compromised there. The more he considered things, the more he realized that he did not become the principal at Huntley because he truly aspired to be a school administrator. He had ended up as the principal at Huntley because the choices available to him that culminated in him attaining that job were the only logical ones available to him at that time. Dan thought he should finally stake out his own claim, and he had an idea.

"Mom, I've been thinking about applying to the doctoral program at Northern Illinois University and eventually becoming a college professor," Dan said.

"Why don't you?" she asked him.

"What would I live on? It's just not possible."

"Dan, I think it's high time you did something you wanted to do. Would you like to come home and stay with me?"

After a slight pause, Dan said, "Mom, can I come home?"

Two seconds later, Dan began to cry and cry like nothing Emma had ever seen before, and he put his head on Emma's lap for a long time. He didn't move as she stroked his hair. He certainly felt thankful for his mother.

After about a half-hour, barely audible, he finally spoke.

"Mom, Dad would be so disappointed if he saw me now. My life is a shambles. I'm a total failure."

"Dan, that's just not true. Your father was a perfectionist, and he beat himself up constantly for nearly everything that didn't work out. He was very demanding of those he held in high regard. It couldn't have been easy for you, I know. But what you don't understand is that he had amazing empathy for all of humanity—especially those who fell short. It tore him up when he watched others suffer. He understood that, and that empathy is probably one of the reasons he was such a good coach. He never gave up on anybody. He understood disappointment, and he understood that anybody who set their sights high was bound to fail some—maybe fail a lot. Sometimes, I thought he was compassionate and forgiving to a fault, but he didn't know how to express it, at least around here. He could never find a way to forgive himself for anything, but with everyone else, he was the most tolerant person I've ever seen."

"That's sure not the way it seemed," Dan managed to say.

"Your father couldn't express himself very well, Dan. But I know your father to the marrow, and I know he was exceptionally proud of you. You were not a failure to him, and he wouldn't think that now, either. He thought of you as a success because you never stopped fighting for your dreams."

Dan felt like a puppy from a rescue shelter that had spent the majority of its existence getting the shit beaten out of it. He was a mess. After about another fifteen minutes of silence, Dan asked, "Mom, do you have *Blood on the Tracks* lying around here anywhere?"

"I will put it on for you."

Chapter 15

And the dirt of gossip blows into my face,
And the dust of rumors covers me.
But if the arrow is straight
And the point is slick,
It can pierce through the dust no matter how thick.
So I'll make my stand
And remain as I am
And bid farewell and not give a damn.

--Bob Dylan
Restless Farewell

Dan sent Dr. Stanley an Email Monday morning stating that his lawyer would be contacting him. Dan's lawyer negotiated a settlement to pay Dan the remainder of his salary until the end of the year. Dan moved in with his mom the next week. Later that spring, he sold his house for $235,000. Houses were still selling at that time. The market hadn't crashed yet. A year later, and Dan might not have been so lucky.

The world was on the brink of a financial crisis. In the early 2000s, fresh off the bursting of the dot.com bubble, a wave of concern about corporate accounting practices swept the country. Two of the biggest examples were WorldCom and Enron. WorldCom, the nation's second largest telecommunications company, filed for bankruptcy in 2002. It had $107 billion in assets, but had $41 billion of debt. It had improperly booked $3.8 billion in expenses, and its CEO resigned amid questions over $366 million in personal loans. The SEC filed civil fraud charges against it for over nine billion dollars worth of accounting errors. Enron, a natural gas pipeline company, in a significant but lesser scandal, filed for bankruptcy in 2003. In 2001, *Fortune Magazine* named it the most innovative company in America for the sixth consecutive year. Turns out, its innovations were illegal. That same year, the federal government announced it was beginning an investigation of the company, and Enron's stock fell fifteen dollars in a single day. By the time all was said and done, the scandal wiped out hundreds of people's savings for retirement and college tuition.

By the middle of the decade, the financial debacle had manifested itself in the housing market. In the Nineties, the Clinton Administration thought it wise to make home loans available to more people and relaxed the laws accordingly. Lenders coaxed people into variable rate and interest-only loans. Lending institutions bundled these loans with other loans to make them feasible. As people started to default on their payments, the lending institutions were, in many cases, as strapped for cash as the people scrambling to make payment. Their inability to accurately account for their assets and liabilities caused Jon Stewart on *The Daily Show* to quip, "You know all that money you've been giving to the banks. They don't have it." Foreclosures ran rampant. Dan even read stories in the paper about renters being evicted when landlords couldn't make payments on their investment properties. All of the businesses that had fed off the housing boom—the makers of furniture, lighting fixtures, electrical appliances, entertainment devices, the shipping industry, etc.—began to suffer, and unemployment began to rise. Banks refused to lend money, credit stopped, and people were either unable or unwilling to buy things. The country fell into a recession.

Dan managed to sell his house before the fallout. This turned out to be a huge break for him—one that he badly needed. The following year, he picked up the newspaper, and while flipping through the pages, noticed a story indicating that Enron's top executives had been found guilty on a variety of counts related to fraud and money laundering.

Loud noises emanated from Emma's brother's house on Christmas Eve. The neighbors were used to the annual wild McBride extravaganza, and Dan couldn't have needed this night more. He spent a lot of time playing with Derek: reading him stories of Santa, rolling around on the floor with him, making it so Dylan and Lisa could actually talk to each other if they wanted. Dan thought the two seemed happy together.

Dylan danced around the subject and finally asked Dan, "Well, what do you think you're going to do?"

"I'm not really sure. I applied to get into the doctoral program at Northern. Right now, I guess I'm hoping that works out," Dan said.

Then he asked, "How's your season going? I have to get out to watch a couple games."

Dylan had been named the head basketball coach at Barrington to replace his father. Dylan's first team was competitive, but he was not as good a coach as his dad (few were), and had been the target recently of some criticism for his team's performance. Dylan didn't seem to be bothered by any of it.

"We'll be okay. We lost a couple in the Thanksgiving Tournament. Everyone got all up in arms. We didn't play very well."

Dan's natural tendency was to come to the defense of his little brother. He tried to turn his response into a joke.

"Want me to dust them back?" Dan was referring to a pitch in which the pitcher, believing that the batter might be taking advantage of the strike zone by standing too close to the plate, intentionally throws inside off the plate to move the hitter farther away from the plate.

Dylan responded with a joke of his own. "I don't think you scare anybody, anymore, Dan."

Then Dylan added, "Dan, don't worry, my friend. If you got that close to pitching in the big leagues and can keep it together after that, I can handle a little flak for losing a couple of high school basketball game, okay?"

In life people do things for other people without knowing it, and, in time, it cuts both ways.

Later that night, Dan called Louise's house to speak with Melinda Sue. He and Anna Jean talked directly as little as possible, but Anna Jean was never difficult regarding their daughter.

"Merry Christmas, Melinda Sue. Did you get my present?"

"I got it, Daddy. I love it. It's my favorite present."

It was a Chicago Cubs stuffed bear.

"Daddy, there's no snow down here. Mommy says you will bring some with you when you come down."

"Yes, well, it would only be too sad when it melts. Maybe it's better if the snow stays up here. How about I come down when the weather gets warm?"

Emma had to leave to sing at Midnight Mass. Dan did not like to go to Midnight Mass, but he did get up and go to church in the morning. He wanted to be someplace familiar, so even though he no longer lived on the south side of Crystal Lake, he went to his former church, St. Elizabeth Ann Seton's. This provided some comfort for him as he sat alone with his thoughts.

Dan went to his mother's on Christmas Day of 2004. The traditional gathering included only him and his mom this year. There was no Don, no Anna Jean, and no Melinda Sue. Dylan, Lisa, and Derek elected to attend the gathering at her mother's house. Her sister was home from college, and Lisa's mom talked them into going over there to meet her new fiance. The Christmas music played in the background. Emma puttered around the various rooms and created smells in the kitchen that permeated throughout the house, reminding Dan of his childhood. Occasionally, Dan got up and grabbed a Sam Adams Winter Lager. Dan loved fires. He found the flickering of the flame and its gentle crackling to be very relaxing. As he looked at it, he remembered how Anna Jean's nutcracker collection had lined up across the top of their fireplace. Everything about the day had a calming effect on Dan, and his mood allowed him to smirk silently at the thought of it.

They read the paper, watched the Christmas movies on television, and talked. Late afternoon, after they had sat down to eat, they exchanged presents.

Emma went first. She got him a Northern Illinois Huskies sweatshirt.

"Dan, I just know you're going to get accepted. I want you to have something to wear!"

"I love it, Mom. It's perfect. This is so you."

Then Dan gave his mom her present.

Emma delicately opened the wrapping paper and stared at the gift for about thirty seconds, though it seemed like forever to Dan.

Dan had given her his game ball from the Georgia Tech game. He had autographed it, bought a ball holder, and had the plate engraved to read, "From Dan to Mom, Game Ball, Georgia vs. Georgia Tech, Feb. 25, 1996, WP—Dan Mason."

Fighting back tears, Emma said, "Dan, I can't take this from you."

"You have to, Mom. I realized the day after Thanksgiving that I threw that game for you."

Emma and Dan, survivors both, had made their peace. Dan learned it was possible to have a woman for a friend.

Chapter 16

If you see her, say hello . . .
Say for me that I'm all right though things get kind of slow
She might think that I've forgotten her, don't tell her it isn't so . . .
We had a falling-out like lovers often will
And to think of how she left that night, it still brings me a chill
And though our separation, it pierced me to the heart
She still lives inside of me, we've never been apart.

--Bob Dylan
If You See Her, Say Hello

The second week of January, in the year 2005, Dan learned that Northern accepted him into its doctoral program. He planned to work toward a degree in Educational Administration. Dan thought he had a pretty good chance at a Teaching Assistant position in Dr. Trent Flanagan's office. Dr. Flanagan was the director of the Office of Research, Evaluation, and Policy Studies, and Dan had developed a positive relationship with him during his previous graduate work.

Fancy title aside, Dr. Flanagan referred to himself simply as a stats guy ("psychometrician" was the fancy word for it). The university considered him a rainmaker. He still taught a little, but he had been gradually relinquishing his classroom duties to become more involved in consulting work for the state and local school districts and municipalities, such as profiling work for the Naperville Police Department. The university approved Dan for the position in his office and began work in the fall. He went to school full time. Most of the people in the program were practicing administrators, so classes were scheduled for Saturdays. During the week, he taught a couple undergraduate courses and assisted Dr. Flanagan in the office, mostly feeding numbers into a computer. For this, he received free tuition and a small annual stipend of $5,500.

Flanagan was an interesting bird, and not everyone took to him. Dan did. He "got" Flanagan. Flanagan became something of a father figure to Dan at a time when he needed it. After Dan got to know him better, he learned that Flanagan was Catholic, served in Vietnam, and occupied a spot well to the right on the political spectrum. Dan discovered the last two after they got to know each other better. Flanagan was also damn good at what he did, and Dan learned a great deal from him. Dr. Flanagan came across as a flake to most people. He would do just about anything for anybody, but unless a person understood his humor, he or she could be left wondering if he truly believed he was still landing helicopters under heavy artillery fire, or if a bottle of Scotch was really the necessary offering to ensure an "A" rather than a "B" in one of his graduate classes.

After Anna Jean got her cut, the profits of the sale of the house went mostly toward Dan's legal fees. By living with his mom, Dan managed to put a little money away. He joined Snap Fitness to stay in shape, and got a bartender license to supplement his income. He found work at the Barrington Brewery. During the school year, he worked mostly on weeknights a couple of times a week. During breaks and summers, he picked up more hours.

Dan decided not to call Duke that summer. He thought it would be easier to seek out some direction in his life if he put baseball on hold for a while. He did not blame himself for the way his baseball career had ended. He had given it his all. Maybe someday, he'd be ready again, but not now. Too much had happened too fast. If he chose to play again, he wanted to experience the pure joy of it. Dan needed to sort through his emotions, and he didn't want baseball to be mixed up in all of that. If and when he played again, he wanted it to be a genuine part of his life, not an escape.

Dan found it to be much more difficult to let Anna Jean go. She had left him, and he couldn't stop thinking that the whole thing must somehow be his fault. Dan carried the note from Thanksgiving week around with him in his wallet. Part of him thought she would think the better of it, and something would happen to bring them back together. By spring of 2006 when their divorce became final, had one peeked into his billfold, they still would have found the note neatly tucked away.

Night after night at the bar, he saw young couples in love and pretty single girls with their friends. Many of those girls were looking at him, and several made suggestive comments to him, but he let them pass. Many knew his story, and some felt sorry for him. Most of the girls in the bar appreciated his sun-weathered good looks or his pleasant, gracious demeanor, or a combination of both. Some who came from local families may not have known much of the events from Huntley but were clearly aware of his status as a local legend. He could have been an appealing find for many girls for any one of a number of reasons, but he had no interest in seeking out a new relationship.

Dan tended bar the way he pitched: precise, smooth, calm, and relaxed. Though he never pitched professionally, from little on, that is how he went about his business on the mound—like a pro, and that is exactly the way he operated behind the bar. However, socially, Dan enjoyed hanging out in bars, especially on bad weather days. He liked feeling that, despite the power of Mother Nature, a mass of humanity sat there huddled together, enjoying this moment in this life together. He enjoyed looking out the window at softly falling snow through the reflection of the Christmas lights. He loved the camaraderie and enjoyed observing how people behaved. He loved the conversation. It reminded him of his days at the Cape and the card games on the bus rides. But he also liked the detachment. Dan had grown a bit gun-shy. He currently enjoyed the connection to the people without the responsibility and commitment required in "the real world." If someone annoyed him, he got up and walked away.

One time, Dan stopped in a place called the Kelsey Roadhouse and began to ponder the concept of community. He recalled the first winter after he and Anna Jean had bought their house. Regularly, several days after a snowstorm, Dan would be out jogging and become extremely frustrated when at least half of the people in his neighborhood had cleared only enough snow to get their cars out of their driveways. They didn't have enough courtesy to even shovel a path. Dan had to constantly dart back out into the street, hoping to avoid traffic. His frustration became anger when he thought of Melinda Sue trudging through all the snow when she walked to school. As soon as it had stopped snowing, Dan shoveled his walk. His parents raised him that way. As Dan contemplated the matter, he realized that, in all likelihood, Barrington did not differ much from Crystal Lake, but people always idealized their childhood, and Dan did not remember it that way. He agreed with Vonnegut's point about the loss of community. It seemed that most people didn't even live in the community they worked in anymore. People immersed themselves into their own children, but missed the larger picture. Dan theorized that the increased mobility of society had something to do with it. He lamented that many kids rarely saw their grandparents, and that stories and family histories did not commonly get passed down to the younger generations the way they once did. His personal thoughts on the matter, of course, changed nothing, and he knew that, considering his current situation, he had no right to talk. He wanted to feel like he belonged to something in this world, so he sought that out where he could find it, and sometimes hanging out at the local gathering places was the closest thing to that feeling available to him.

Dan worked for Dr. Flanagan for a total of three years. During that time, he went to Georgia to see Melinda Sue over spring break. In the summer, she came north to see him.

Her first visit was the summer of 2005.

"Isn't it funny, Daddy, that you live with your mommy, and I live with my mommy?" she said.

Dan said he didn't really think it was so funny, but certainly she could think so if she wanted to.

Chapter 17

Most of the time . . .
I don't even notice she's gone . . .
I can survive, I can endure
And I don't even think about her . . .
Most of the time
I'm strong enough not to hate . . .
Don't even remember what her lips felt like on mine . . .
Most of the time.

--Bob Dylan
Most of the time

Dan plugged away at his coursework. Most Sundays, he went to church at St. Anne's with his mom. He returned to the mound in the summer of 2006, pitching on weekends for Lombard and occasionally on weeknights if the games didn't conflict with the nights the Brewery scheduled him to tend bar. The fall term got off to a good start. He continued working for Flanagan and desperately tried to get his head around the type of study he wanted to conduct for his dissertation.

That year, Dylan released *Modern Times*, his first number-one album since 1976's *Desire*. The album's title mimics a 1936 Charlie Chaplain film, and its themes were consistent with Dylan's recent fascination of going back in time, connecting past to present, and portraying a traditional Americana with a truly unique blend of traditional music: rock, swing, rockabilly—everything at once. It included "Workingman's Blues #2", a beautiful song, perfectly delivered. Dan considered that song as good as anything Bob had ever done. He preferred *Modern Times*' predecessor *Love and Theft* for its harder-driving blues sound but thoroughly enjoyed the new album, nonetheless.

Dan made slow but sure progress on his dissertation, but all the while he could not get Anna Jean out of his head. He figured she would be fine, if for no other reason than the fact that she possessed incredible good looks. She had moved out of her mother's house that summer. Though she had readjusted well to Georgia and liked being more proximal to her mother, she still could not stomach the thought of living in Swainsboro forever. She didn't have too many options, but had a few friends in Athens. She had visited them periodically and learned of a job opening at the Athens Regional Medical Center.

Anna Jean had the background for the position and decided to apply. They offered her the job and she accepted. Anna Jean made the move to Athens, where she secured an apartment. This enabled her to visit her mother frequently and live somewhere familiar in a place not named Swainsboro. Now, more accustomed to the bigger city, she ventured into Atlanta occasionally for some shopping with her friends, to take Melinda Sue to the Fulton County Zoo, or other similar mini-adventures.

In February of 2007, Dan called Anna Jean to make arrangements for his March visit with Melinda Sue. The past two years, Dan had picked her up in Swainsboro. He needed to confirm directions to her place and wanted to make sure the dates he suggested would work. Dan blew all of his money on these trips. The first year he and Melinda Sue had visited Atlanta, gone to some Georgia baseball games, and taken a drive to Savannah. Last year, he had taken her to Hilton Head, South Carolina. He had left a message, expecting Anna Jean to call him back. Three days later, he received a letter.

Chapter 18

Accidentally, like a martyr
The hurt gets worse and the heart gets harder

--Warren Zevon
Accidentally, Like a Martyr

The letter read:

> *Dear Dan,*
>
> *I moved two weeks ago. My new address is 3558 Ranier Drive, in Atlanta. I met a man at work this fall, and we plan to be married this summer. He is the Head Surgeon for the Cardiac Vascular Center at the hospital.*
>
> *Oh, Dan, it all happened so fast, and I just didn't know how to tell you. I meant to call, but then you called, and I just didn't know what to do. It didn't seem to make sense to keep the apartment, so I moved here with him.*
>
> *Melinda Sue is very excited and gets along well with his two kids when they come to visit. There is a boy, age 12, and a girl Melinda Sue's age (she would be ten in June). Melinda Sue can't wait until it gets a little warmer and she can go swimming in the pool.*
>
> *The dates you left on the message work fine. Please let me know the time you plan to arrive. You can Google the directions. If you have any questions on how to find us, let me know.*
>
> *Love,*
>
> *Anna Jean*

Dan looked up the address. Buckhead! Unbelievable. The girl of his dreams was sucking another man's cock and fucking his doctor brains out . . . in a million dollar house . . . in BUCKHEAD!

Still, for no logical reason whatsoever, he kept the note in his wallet.

True to form, they were married that summer. Anna Jean Simpson Mason was now Anna Jean Taylor, one half of the formidable Dr. and Mrs. Taylor, and one helluva cocktail party hostess, no pun intended.

In the fall of 2007, Dan got the first three chapters of his dissertation approved. He conducted his study on teacher compensation. Dr. Flanagan helped him generate his stats for his study, and in February, 2008, he successfully defended his dissertation and officially became, Dr. Mason.

Too little, too late.

Dan thought a lot about the crossroads he faced and the journey that had brought him to this point. He theorized that being a man meant developing the capacity to accept the randomness of fate and somehow still be left loving humanity.

Dan had completed his doctorate and had begun to apply for full-time entry level professor positions, but so far nothing had materialized. He decided to see Doug in Florida, and then swing back up for his visit with Melinda Sue. He thought it would be good to see Doug and be someplace else for a while. A lot had happened in the three years since Doug had retired. He had settled in the Sarasota area on the Gulf side, a bit south of the Tampa-St. Petersburg area. The Reds trained there. They took in a few spring training games. With Bob on tour in South America, there would be no Dylan concert to see, so they mostly sat outside, enjoyed the weather, and listened to Dylan on the stereo while drinking bottles of Landshark beer.

Dan returned from his visit with Doug and Melinda Sue rested but no more enlightened on what might come next than when he had left. A week after he had returned, his phone rang. It was Dr. Victoria Chou, Dean of the College of Education at the University of Illinois-Chicago.

"May I speak with Dr. Mason, please?"

"This is he."

"Dr. Mason, this is Dr. Chou from UIC."

"Good morning, Dr. Chou." Dan's enthusiasm couldn't have been more obvious.

"Dr. Kevin Kumashiro, Department Chair for Educational Policy Studies, is recommending you for the assistant professor position. Will you accept?"

"I happily accept."

"Outstanding. Dr. Flanagan spoke very highly you. I am sure you are the perfect fit."

It was a tenure track position with an annual salary of $65,000. Dan could supplement that by writing, presenting, and consulting, which most college professors did, but it would likely take him a while before that became a reality. Three years after he had quit a $100,000 job and tussled as a bartender to receive the highest degree possible, he was back to an entry level position, making almost $35,000 a year less than he had as principal at Huntley. Yet, Dan felt exhilarated with his new purpose in life. I'll live in the city! I'm alive! He couldn't help himself and blurted out loud, "I have my life back!"

Dan sent a bottle of Scotch to Dr. Flanagan, and later that evening, when his mom had gotten back from running some errands, he told her the news. Emma spontaneously burst into tears of joy and lurched forward to hug her son.

The first time Dan had left home, in the summer of 1995, he had thought he had left for good. He could not have been more mistaken. The false security of youth had led him to that conclusion. It is a sad fact that people make the most significant decisions of their lives at very young ages when they are least capable of doing so and know next to nothing. For many athletes, this is magnified even more. Dan had experienced a great deal at a very young age.

One year after he had left, Dan had come back with his young family to live with his parents, and nine years after that, he came back yet again. His third stay at his home in Barrington lasted three whole years. It allowed him to mend fences with his mother, and in the face of tremendous heartache, he did not break. Emma would not let him.

Dan said, "Mom, I have to leave. I've been thinking about it, and it's time."

"Of course you do, Dan. I lived my whole life knowing I'd have to let you go. I am just so thankful to God that you and I had the time we did. This time, my son is going out to start his life. That is so much different than a stranger walking out my door."

Just as Dan was finally ready to go it alone, his mom was finally ready to let him go.

Chapter 19

Walking through the leaves, falling from the trees
Feeling like a stranger, nobody sees
So many things that we never will undo
I know you're sorry, I'm sorry too

--Bob Dylan
Mississippi

In 2008, the big blockbuster movie was *Sex and the City*, and Dan had to endure the massive hype that came along with it. Articles appeared in every paper, every publication, and every news outlet imaginable. Dan couldn't ride an exercise bike at Snap Fitness without the talking heads on CNN extolling the greatness of the film and its monumental significance.

Because he knew that Anna Jean had liked the show and would probably see the movie, he paid attention to almost everything said and written about the film. One article in the *Chicago Tribune* explained that one of the episodes of the show had discussed the relative merits of people pissing on each other.

It was then he took the note out of his wallet. He went to the kitchen, where he kept the matches that he used to start the grill. He lit the edge of the note and watched the paper start to blacken and shrivel until gradually the flame worked its way to the other edge of the note. Finally, all he could see was the "L" from "Love" and the "A" from "Anna Jean," and, just like that, the note disappeared forever.

The whole thing took about two seconds, but there was an almost surreal stoppage of time in which Dan's life replayed itself—the flame, a supernova—and just when the "L" and the "A" disintegrated for good, so, too, did Dan's last remnant of pain.

People steal things from other people all the time. They steal their youth, their innocence, their hope, their money, and in severe cases, their futures. They do it consciously and subconsciously. When one loses something of value, one frequently perceives it as having been stolen, whether this is accurate or not. This transference is comforting. It allows the person to shift the blame to another, fair or unfair. The distinction between loss and theft is so subtle that often neither thief nor victim can ascertain the difference. In this context, it makes perfect sense to believe in salvation through a higher being. No matter how well-meaning one party may be, what can forgiveness between mutual perpetrators actually be worth in this world? The forgiver, at some point, has inevitably stolen something from another, knowingly or otherwise. The one undeniable constant is that which is gone, is gone, never to return—lost or stolen, it does not matter. Value can be seen through the eyes of both thief and victim, but loss can only be processed through the senses of the victim, the one who has lost something of perceived value. Fault becomes irrelevant at that point. The victim must let it go or go crazy. Some think they've let it go, but being unaware that they really haven't, spend the majority of their time trying to keep from losing their mind.

Goodbye, Anna Jean, Dan said to himself among the ashes. To the best of my ability, goodbye.

That fall, Dan, thoroughly rejuvenated with his new position at UIC, began another chapter in his life. He poured everything he had into his new position. He took the train around town, going to a Cubs game and taking in a show at The House of Blues, among other things.

The excitement and constant buzz of the city pulsed through him. Every night, he looked around at the lights and let them soak through his skin. Thoroughly invigorated, Dan felt alive! He had not felt this way since the day they had handed him his gear his freshman year at Georgia, when his dreams were in front of him, and he had been saturated with hope.

Dylan called Dan in mid-September and said he had an extra ticket to the Northwestern-Michigan State football game on October 11. Would Dan like to go? It was the perfect call at the perfect time.

They made the trip to Evanston, where Dan had seen Bob Dylan for the first time. Dylan and his family were doing fine. Derek was starting kindergarten this year, and Lisa was expecting again around the holidays.

On the way to the game, Dan espied a young couple so obviously in love that even he noticed. He assumed that he and Anna Jean had looked that way one day fourteen years ago. For a second, he wondered if the couple had any clue what lie ahead of them, but he knew they did not. Nobody ever did. He said a quick prayer, wishing them luck.

Dan knew Melinda Sue would be in that spot someday. He began to think about his daughter. He wondered if they could ever share the moments he and his mother had, if she would ever know him, if she would even care that he could once throw a ball. He hoped that maybe someday she might even attend the college where he taught, but he never mentioned this to her.

While walking through the picturesque autumn campus, with colored leaves falling to the ground everywhere, the bitterness inside of Dan began to recede. On his own but not alone, he had his family; a career he was passionate about; and a healthy, vibrant daughter. He had been going to church most Sundays—sometimes he even took the train out, listened to his mom sing in the choir, and spent the day with her. Frequently, he made something on the grill; other times, she made a meal. They watched football or baseball on TV, and Dan often thought about the ominous day he had chosen sides.

He pondered his future, still unaware of what might lie ahead. Maybe he'd write a book someday. Suddenly, he was becoming himself again, full of dreams.

Dan's definition of being a man continued to evolve. Perhaps it had nothing at all to do with coming to grips with the randomness of fate. Recently, he had begun to lean more toward the "every hair is numbered" side. He started to believe that, even though he had no idea what it could be, God had a plan for him.

Dan got back from the Northwestern game, went over to his stereo to pick out a CD, and suddenly had an idea. He picked up the phone and called his mom.

"Mom, any chance I can stop by tomorrow afternoon?"

"Sure can. You coming to church or coming over after?"

"I'll be by around one o'clock."

Dan arrived and handed her a UIC Flames sweatshirt. She said she would wear it this winter when she took the train in to see some college basketball games.

"Hey, Mom, Bob is playing in Milwaukee on November 6th. Would you like to go with me? I think Dad would like that."

"Dan, I would appreciate the second chance. Thanks so much for asking."

Bob had recently released *Tell Tale Signs*, a collection of alternative versions of songs, previously unreleased songs, and live versions of songs. It included some material from the *Time Out of Mind* recording sessions, free of the over-production favored by Lanois. The tour did not feature any songs from the album, but the compilation was a gem. One couldn't help wonder how much more stuff Dylan and Sony were sitting on.

Emma was fifty-eight when she experienced Bob for the first time. She heard "Thunder on the Mountain", "Love Minus Zero/ No Limits", "Lonesome Day Blues", "A Hard Rains A-Gonna Fall', "Tweedle Dee and Tweedle Dum", "Girl from the North Country", "High Water (for Charlie Patton)", "Workingman Blues #2", "Just Like a Woman", "Tangled Up in Blue", "Love Sick", "Highway 61 Revisited", "Ain't Talking", "Summer Days", "Like a Rolling Stone", "All Along the Watchtower", and "Blowin' in the Wind".

Dan couldn't tell if his mom liked the concert. Emma didn't really know what to make of it, which is perhaps the point. A Bob concert would certainly mirror life effectively if it were.

That month, Bush's approval rating was up (yes, up) to twenty-six percent from twenty percent. During his final visit to Iraq, scheduled to celebrate the success of a recent troop surge, an Iraqi reporter threw his shoes at the president, an Arabic gesture of ultimate contempt.

The election of 2008 was a choice between Barack Obama, a senator from Illinois, and Hillary Clinton. Obama won the primary against Clinton, and technically had to beat McCain to win the presidency. However, the country simply could not bring itself to vote for another Republican after the fiasco that was the Bush Administration. For one thing, McCain was a hawk, and, at least for the time being, America was sick of war. For another, he appeared a tad out of touch with the times. He was a technophobe who, when asked during a campaign stop, could not recall how many houses he owned. The answer was seven. So, the primary was the election. Though polar opposites in ideology, Obama captured the imagination of the country similar to the way Reagan had twenty-eight years prior. He spoke a positive message of hope for America. Obama named Clinton Secretary of State. For her part, she refused to go away.

Obama had his hands full. The economy, in its worst shape since the Great Depression, sat at the top of the list of problems. In response, just prior to Obama taking office in January, Congress authorized a $700 billion dollar bailout of the financial industry, money which AIG and other companies used to pay executives bonuses, some in excess of one million dollars. The companies seemed not to understand the public's dissatisfaction with that decision. Next, the car companies came with their hands out. Mired by years of bad labor contracts and poor management, they claimed to be on the verge of collapse. Between their deaf ears and the Bush Administration's ties to the oil industry, no one seemed to want to listen to Thomas Friedman when he tried to explain to everyone that the world is hot, flat, and crowded. Despite what the science community told the populace, the country found denying that Greenland was dissolving into the Atlantic Ocean to be more convenient. It deemed building gas-guzzling SUV's, essentially giving American money to oil-rich countries like Saudi Arabia, bin Laden's birth-place, which enslaved women while ensuring its princes lived luxurious lives, preferable.

Detroit eventually got its money.

Back in the day, when Dan had encountered his financial difficulties, no one suggested a bailout for him an appropriate solution to his problems.

The Sunday before Christmas Eve, Dan read the paper. It was bursting with news. The financial bailout dominated the news, as did another story. The decision to give the money to the auto industry came a couple of days after news outlets reported that Bernard L. Madoff had allegedly defrauded investors of $50 billion, give or take, in a gigantic Ponzi scheme that had been going on since at least 2005. The SEC reportedly ignored multiple warnings of irregularities. Once again, thousands of people's savings were completely wiped out. Charitable foundations were decimated. Closer to home, Illinois Governor Rod Blagojevich, already embroiled in a Federal investigation, recently had been arrested at his home for trying to sell Obama's senate seat. Illinois was a legendarily corrupt state, and the Chicago Tribune was having a field day with that story.

Dan thought, "*These people are trying to tell us how to run schools?*" Then he thought, *You know what? Maybe, all things considered, I did okay. I can say I did my best, anyway. What more can a person say than that? Look at the craziness! I tried my best to pitch in the big leagues, and I got hurt. All right, I can accept that it didn't work out. I can't help it that I got hurt. But I also did my best to keep my marriage together and raise my daughter. I thought I could control that, but how can one control another's happiness? How could I have stopped Kim Masterson from lying? How could I have stopped Anna Jean from getting on that plane? How could I have made any more money than I did? I'm not the government. I can't print my own money!* For the first time ever, Dan stopped blaming himself. If events had played out even slightly differently, the one decision that was truly his to make—the decision to attend Georgia rather than sign—could have been a masterstroke. He could have been one in a million: a big league pitcher with a beautiful wife. Who's to say what might have happened if he had signed? *Nope. I don't regret it.* Even at this moment, Dan could not be sure what he could or couldn't control. There was just too much confusion.

That month, Bob Dylan announced dates for a spring tour of Europe, and Dan didn't know if he and his mom would ever get another chance to see a show together. But when he went over to his uncle's house on Christmas Eve for the annual McBride extravaganza and blowout, Dan brought her a copy of *Rolling Stone* and showed her an article in which they had rated Dylan the seventh greatest singer of all-time.

A little later in the evening, he seized a break in the action and walked over to her.

"Hey, Mom,"

She cut him off.

"It's okay, Dan, I can drive myself to church later."

This was good because Dan had already tossed back a couple Black Russians.

"Oh, well, that's good, but that's not what I wanted. Read this. An Irish guy wrote it. I thought you said Bob couldn't sing."

Bono, the lead singer of U2, wrote the tribute:

"His closet won't close for all the shoes of the characters that walk through his stories . . . The voice becomes the words . . . There is no performing, just life—as Yeats says, when the dancer becomes the dance . . . Dylan did with singing what Brando did with action. He busted through the artifice to get to the art. Both of them tore down the prissy rules laid down by the schoolmarms of their craft, broke through the fourth wall, got in the audience's face and said, 'I dare you to think I'm kidding.'"

"Well, maybe I was wrong," Emma said.

"Wrong, Mom. Wrong. Did you just say you were wrong?" Dan said through his laughter.

"I'll never admit it," she said as she blushed.

Unexpectedly, in the spring of 2009, Dylan released yet another album of original songs entitled *Together through Life*. His thirty-third studio album featured an additional instrument: the accordion. The more one listened to this record, the better it got. These songs, while steeped in the traditions on display in his previous albums, were simultaneously edgy and calming and managed to evoke images of previous times while striking the listener as thoroughly contemporary. Dylan announced a summer tour with Willie Nelson and John Mellencamp, and, in April, Dan called his mom.

"Mom, I don't know what you think of this, but Bob's playing up in Milwaukee at Summerfest on July 1. Any chance you might be interested in going? A lot of times, it's the second show when people start to like it."

"Why, I would be delighted," she said.

Dan and Emma saw Bob again together.

In the movie *Field of Dreams*, James Earl Jones says, "Baseball has marked the time, Ray."

But so had another. Sixty-seven year old Bob Dylan not only marked the time, but he chronicled it like no other.

Dan often recalled something his psychology teacher had done his junior year in high school. He drew a circle on the board and said this is your life. He drew a line down the middle and said, "These are the first two years of your life." Then he drew an intersecting line dividing the circle again and said, "These are the first four years of your life." He did that a couple more times before he stopped. How true, Dan thought. How true.

Dan, thirty-four, entertained the possibility that he might catch his second wind soon, similar to someone else he admired. In Love and Theft's "Summer Days", Bob sings, "The girls all say, 'You're a worn out star' . . . She says, 'You can't repeat the past.' I say, 'You can't? What do you mean you can't? Of course you can.'"

Chapter 20

I'm just gonna let you pass,
Yes, and I'll go last.
Then time will tell who fell
And who's been left behind,
When you go your way and I go mine.

--Bob Dylan
Most Likely You Go Your Way (and I'll Go Mine)

For the most part, Dan adjusted to his new life rather well. He visited Doug in Florida every other year and channeled his energy into his job. He tried in every way to rid himself of the torment of the loss of Anna Jean, but a dull ache for her manifested itself all too frequently. Some days, he felt exhausted and heavy, as if his entire being just sank into whatever piece of furniture he happened to be sitting on, and it took all he could do to get up—even for a beer. Other times, his neck got stiff and his temples hurt. He tried to figure out why this had been happening and deduced that his subconscious life was playing games with him. He realized that these episodes coincided with various times of the year, such as late June, when Anna Jean had visited him at the Cape, or October, when she had accepted his proposal, or November when she had left him, or March when he had discovered that she had found another man. To the extent possible, he started to take precautions against the inevitable, stocking up on ibuprofen (and beer), making plans to go to concerts or visit his mom to try to take his mind off Anna Jean. He thought he had let go; he tried to let go; but in reality, he could not let go. When the time came, Dan found it far easier to let go of baseball, which he realized all players had to do at some point, than to deal with the idea of Anna Jean loving somebody else.

Dan kept himself in pretty good shape, and in the summers of 2009 and 2010, he once again joined the Lombard team. Lombard played a few games at Les Miller Field on the UIC campus. The Sears Tower, now the Willis Tower, formed a magnificent backdrop in centerfield, especially for night games. Dan attended every game during those two seasons, helped Duke manage a little, worked with the younger pitchers, and, for the first time in a long time, felt part of a team: a *family*—a *community*. When in Sheboygan, he made sure to say hello to Dana, who had instructed him on the fine craft of preparing the perfect brat, whenever he could. His arm felt pretty good. He posted a 26-6 cumulative won-loss record over those two summers. Dan retired from baseball for good at the age of thirty-six. Melinda Sue came up to visit each summer and saw her father pitch. In the process, she began to understand him better. Dan began calling her Lindy, partially because he had grown weary of women with two first names. Melinda Sue liked the nickname, mostly because nobody else called her that—it was just between them.

As Lindy grew older, she thought back on the visits with her dad and concluded that he was not a bad man at all. In fact, she considered him a good man who, in many ways, without being immature, possessed many qualities of a little boy in a way that she found pleasing. When he played, she could sense his vitality. She could see the dreamer in him and wondered what he might have been like as a young man. She began to understand how her mom had fallen in love with him. It would have been an easy thing to do. Emma saw Dan pitch several times a year, and Dylan, Lisa, and their family—now grown to three children—did also. The little ones took pride in Uncle Dan. Dylan told them many stories of how good Dan really was, back in the day.

Dan could have continued to play, but he chose not to. Duke lobbied him to throw, but Dan declined. The Illinois State Board of Education asked Dan to serve on a state commission on teacher compensation. President Obama had named Arne Duncan, the former CEO of the Chicago Public Schools, Secretary of the Department of Education, and together they crafted a platform to improve teacher quality and reform teacher compensation, both areas of expertise for Dan. Despite the fact that unions, especially teachers unions, were very powerful in the state, Illinois decided to lead the charge. Progress ranged from slow to non-existent, and, if anything, it reinforced what Dan already knew: he did not like politics. However, Dan believed in the cause, so he stuck with it. All of this consumed a great deal of his time. Single districts required several years to change the way they paid their teachers. At the state level, the process was even more cumbersome.

Dan made his peace with his mom, and now he set his mind at ease about his baseball career. After those two summers of being on a team again, he did not want to be a part-time gun for hire. He wanted either to be a true member of the team, or he wanted to move on with his life. He had spent ten years holding on to half a dream, and still had not completely let go. That part of his life remained rather painful, and he did not want it to be that way with baseball. Dan decided that, if he could not totally immerse himself in baseball, he had to let it go. He could control that. He did not want to associate regret, remorse, melancholy, or any other bittersweet or upsetting emotion with baseball. He wanted to remember himself as a baseball player—the one who had been awarded a scholarship to Georgia, who had pitched in the Cape Cod League, who had beaten Georgia Tech, and who had proved at thirty-five he could still throw—and he wanted that memory to be pure. In addition to his work for the university and the state, Dan kept busy writing, presenting, and consulting with other school districts about their school improvement efforts. Over time, he became very well known in the Chicago-land area for his work in these areas. On the side, he toiled away, trying to write a book that he hoped people would consider worth reading. Anybody, he thought—just one person. Though he had been known since his youth as a very good writer, and though he wrote regularly as part of his work, he had never written fiction. The creative process and all that went into it was a different animal. He read a great deal, but when he read his own writing back to himself, he could tell that he had not accomplished what he had set out to do. He truly believed that somewhere inside of him resided a story to share.

While at UIC, Dan attended the baseball games regularly. The Flames were in the Horizon League, and often won their conference, qualifying for the NCAA Regional. Les Miller Field, an all-turf field, was very nice but did not have much seating. When Dan went to the games, he frequently stood upon the right field line: the Flames side.

Dan taught graduate students working toward their master's degrees in educational administration, or needing some foundational classes as they pursued other graduate degrees in the school of education. Dan taught some full time graduate students, who worked on campus as he once did as a doctoral candidate, but more commonly, his students were practicing administrators, balancing work and family, as Dan had done when he pursued his master's degree. Those classes met in the evenings. Once, though, by fluke of schedule, the department assigned Dan an undergraduate course in assessment. In that course, he encountered a struggling student by the name of Randy Wilkerson, who missed frequently (sometimes due to baseball). Dan had multiple conversations with Randy about his academic performance, and when Randy's attitude and quality of work did not improve, Dan contacted Mike Denison, the baseball coach.

"Baseball office, Coach Denison," Mike said in the matter-of-fact way that he answered the phone.

"Coach, this is Dan Mason. I am a professor here at the school, and I have one of your players, Randy Wilkerson, in class. I need to talk with you about his academic performance."

"Mason. Is there some reason why that name should be familiar?" Mike asked.

"I shoot a little money your way. I used to play, and I like to stop by the games once in a while when I can."

"That must be it. I'm pretty good at remembering the names on the checks," Mike said.

"Yeah, I'll bet. So anyway, about Wilkerson . . ."

Mike cut him off. "Why don't you stop by the office, and we can meet. You can tell me what's going on. What's tomorrow look like?"

"Tomorrow works. Morning, I assume, due to practice?"

"Sure, make it ten."

"Ten it is."

Dan stopped over, filled him in, and that day, before practice, Mike and his staff called Wilkerson in to the office, berated him mercilessly, suspended him for a couple games, and from then on, his attendance picked up. Wilkerson, a good player but not a draftable player, barely made it through the class, and both Dan and Mike felt good the following spring when Randy completed all his requirements to graduate, with the exception of his student teaching, which he completed the following fall.

That chance meeting launched a great friendship, and, in the fall, Mike invited Dan into the program to throw batting practice. Dan agreed to come around when he could, but something as simple as that had to be run through the NCAA. It ruled that, though Dan served in no official coaching capacity, he would have to be classified as a volunteer assistant coach. Dan declined rather than take the spot of a young aspiring coach, who would be glad to get paid nothing to be considered a part of the staff. Dan swung over to the field to watch practice on occasion, and one time Mike walked over to him and asked if he'd like to stop out for a beer when they finished up.

Dan consented. Mike suggested they head to Addiction on Lake Street to watch the Cubs game and partake of the 25-cent wings special. *Baseball, wings, beer—not much of a decision*, Dan thought.

After they had found a spot, Dan asked, "So, where'd you go to school Mike?"

"Which time?"

"Well, I pitched at Georgia. Where did you play?"

"I graduated from Southeast Missouri State."

"Cape Girardeau, right?"

"Yep."

"You didn't start out there, though?"

"No, I went to East Mississippi Community College for two years."

"Where is that?"

"Scooba."

"Scooba? Where the hell is that?"

"It's literally in the middle of nowhere, at the intersection of Highways 45 and 16, near the Alabama border. Six hundred people in the whole town."

"You don't sound like a southerner. Why in the world did you pick East Mississippi?"

"Oh, there are reasons, I guess." After a brief pause, Mike continued, "UW-Milwaukee talked to me, but I wanted a place to play where I could end up at a Division I school in the south. I'm from Appleton, Wisconsin. The opportunities up there are limited. I went there to play ball for two years. That's what I did, and then I left for 'SEMO.'"

"Well, I guess I understand that. I wanted to go south, too."

"How did you end up at Georgia?" Mike asked.

Dan told bits and pieces of his story. Some of the details about Anna Jean, the injury, Kim Masterson, and everything else came out over time. However, most of the time, Mike and Dan simply shot the shit, as guys sometimes call it, about baseball and eventually music. The target on Mike's back read, "Next Dylan Convert," and Dan subtly nudged him into the abyss, though he would not see a concert, as Dylan no longer toured.

When it appeared that Dan had closed the tale of his journey to Georgia, Mike jumped in.

"It's a shame about the baseball up north," he said, and then proceeded to explain some of the difficulties facing prospects in his home state.

Appleton was one of the stronger areas in the state for high school baseball, but players in Wisconsin had to overcome a variety of disadvantages that even a kid like Dan from Barrington had not been subject to. In some parts of the state, it took forever for spring to come, and for that reason, some schools played high school baseball in the summer, limiting the number of games for the young players, as well as their exposure. Fortunately, Appleton had spring baseball and a strong Legion program in the summer, so Mike had been able to play in decent programs against some of the better competition around and had been seen by college and professional scouts. However, climate presented only one of the challenges facing aspiring baseball players in the state.

Mike explained that limited collegiate opportunities in the state compounded the problem. Of the four Division I schools in the state, only Wisconsin-Milwaukee had a college baseball program. Wisconsin, of the Big Ten, embarrassed the state in 1991, dropping its program for Title IX reasons. Somehow, its conference counterparts found ways to work around the issue, including schools just as far north or farther, such as Michigan, Michigan State, and Minnesota. Wisconsin-

Green Bay and Marquette, the other Division I schools, did not offer baseball.

Wisconsin-Parkside, a Division II school, had a program, but all of the remaining state universities were classified as Division III and could not award athletic scholarships. These colleges, despite enrollments of 10,000 or 12,000 students, or sometimes even more, competed at the Division III level, often against much smaller private schools. Many good players left the state in search of a Division I opportunity, a scholarship, or an opportunity farther south, but even those who remained and participated in some of the better programs—such as Wisconsin-Oshkosh, Wisconsin-Whitewater, or Wisconsin-Stevens Point—were restricted to thirty-six games, further limiting their development and exposure.

Mike concluded his commentary by saying, "You know, I would have gone to Wisconsin, if they'd had a team. I could have gotten in. But I convinced my parents to let me try it down south for a year to see what happened, and once I did that, things just played out a certain way."

This issue so upset Mike growing up, knowing that he could never play ball for his state school, that frequently, when the mood struck, and always after a few beverages, he reminded Dan of this travesty in the Badger state.

Their easy, comfortable conversation caused them to lose track of time, and they continued to take turns buying rounds.

"So, Mike, when did you decide you wanted to be a coach?"

"Well, I didn't get drafted and was short a few credits to graduate, so I stayed on at SEMO as a student assistant while I finished my degree. I could play circles around everybody, but you know how it goes. I played short my whole life because I made every play, but for the scouts, I had a second baseman's arm. I didn't have the power for that, considering I only ran a seven-flat sixty. They took a pass."

Mike stood about five-foot ten and oozed intensity. Dan could see it all very clearly. Mike had out-hustled everyone his entire life and probably had out-played them all, too. But too many times, the scouts became so obsessed with a player's "tools," that their actual performance took a back seat. The average major league baseball player runs the sixty-yard dash in 6.9 seconds or less. Most middle infielders are faster than that, and although exceptions can be made, those exceptions better hit with power. Mike became just another one of those really good players who would never get a chance to play professional baseball.

Mike had led a rather transient life. Dan learned that, after his stint at SEMO, Mike had taken a graduate assistantship at Southern Illinois University in Carbondale for two years. From there, he had taken a part-time assistant coaching position at Eastern Illinois University in Charleston for two more years. After that, it had been on to Parkland College, a junior college in Champaign, Illinois, where he had accepted the head coaching position. He had stayed there for four years and finally gotten his shot at a Division I coaching job at UIC.

The time had come to head out, and as they wrapped things up, Dan asked, "Mike, you know, we're so close to Greektown. Did you ever head up to the Parthenon to eat? It's right up Halstead."

"No, the closest I've been is the Spectrum Bar and Grill, but I don't eat there. I don't think I'd like Greek food."

The Spectrum featured a bizarre mix of Greek fare and sports and music. Dan conceived of it as a type of Greek Sports Bar, if such a thing existed.

"Mike, you have to try it. Come on. The next time we go out, we're going to try it."

Mike continued to resist as they walked out the door and throughout the cab ride home, but Dan's persistence paid off, and finally Mike relented.

The next weekend, Dan dragged Mike to the Parthenon. Greek music played in the background as the host led them to their seats. Dan convinced Mike to try the Roditas, a red wine that Grandpa Mason used to call "Kool Aid".

"My grandparents and parents used to take us here every time we came to the city. They'd drink a couple bottles of this and, in no time, my dad and grandpa would be cackling away, telling stories, and before you know it, you'd think they were going to beat each other up arguing over the check," Dan said.

Dan ordered Saganaki.

"What's that?" Mike asked.

"You'll see."

A few minutes later, the waiter came back with trays on his arm, poured brandy on the feta cheese, lit it on fire, sprinkled lemon juice on the flames, and said, "Oopa!."

"Try it, Mike."

"You're insane. I haven't had enough of the Kool Aid for that."

"Oh, try it."

Mike did and actually liked it.

They ordered the Loin of Lamb, and talked while they waited for their food.

"You know, Dan, if you never had Wilkerson in class, we wouldn't be sitting here right now."

"Yeah, and if I never heard voices, we might not be sitting here, either."

Mike looked up at him with a quizzical expression on his face, "What's that supposed to mean?"

"Well, it's kind of hard to explain. Maybe another time."

Their meal ended, and Mike agreed that he would come back, but he said, "Next weekend it's my turn. You ever been to the WestEnd Bar and Grill on Madison?"

Dan said he had not.

"We're going. I'll call."

The next weekend, they headed out to WestEnd, Mike told stories, and Dan ate them up.

Mike had made a whole life of coaching. He was wired for coaching, and it meant everything to him. Dan loved listening to him tell his stories, dreaming of the life in baseball that had passed him by. Mike, thirty-six, in his fourth season as the UIC head baseball coach, was on the verge of setting a personal record for staying in one place. He had recruited a full cycle of players, and Dan felt certain that Mike would likely leave soon for a bigger program in a better conference, if the right opportunity presented itself.

Later that evening, Mike, who had a tendency to seek out the companionship of women, struck up a conversation with a friendly member of the opposite sex. Perhaps Dan's bartender instincts took over, but it didn't take him long to figure out where this was leading, and he arranged for a cab ride home solo. This happened a couple times over the next several months, and plenty of similar opportunities availed themselves to Dan. However, Dan wanted no part of that scene. Eventually Mike realized that, and he found somebody else to go out with on the nights that he sensed a stronger likelihood that he might get "distracted." Occasionally, though, Mike succumbed to the temptation when out with Dan, and when that happened, he termed it an "accident."

"Dan, I swear, how was I supposed to know? What was I supposed to do?" etc., etc., and Dan usually laughed it off, unless for some reason something happened that was particularly annoying, in which case Mike took a different tact and simply apologized immediately.

Dan wasn't immune to these impulses. After one of those solo cab rides home, Dan got back to his place and turned on the TV. One of those commercials for the little blue pills came on. At the end, it cautioned, "If you have an erection lasting more than four hours, call your doctor." Dan thought, "If I ever have an erection lasting over four hours, I might place a phone call, but it wouldn't be to my doctor." He made that remark to Dylan once, and Dylan said he thought he heard Jay Leno say that on The Tonight Show.

"Dylan, I always watched Letterman," Dan said. "I swear to you, I thought I made that up all by myself."

Chapter 21

You can't always get what you want
But if you try sometimes you might find
You get what you need

--The Rolling Stones
You Can't Always Get What You Want

By November of 2014, Dan had turned the big "four-oh", and the leaves had changed colors and begun to fall off of the trees. Any Indian summer had come and gone, and one could easily feel the initial bite of Chicago winter in the air. Dan had been fighting off a headache for the past couple days when he received some good and unexpected news. Lindy surprised him with an uncustomary mid-week phone call.

"Dad, I got accepted to UIC. I'm going to go to college at UIC."

Lindy had made several trips to Chicago and did not share her mother's phobia of large cities or the north. Dan was shocked.

"Dad, Dad . . .?"

"Yes, yes."

"I wanted it to be a surprise!"

"You succeeded!"

"Dad, I'm sick of missing you so much all the time. I hope you like having me around, but honestly, I am doing this for me. I want to come by you. You'll have me?"

"Oh, Lindy, you certainly did inherit your mother's ability to get to me," said Dan, fighting back tears.

It took all the energy Dan could muster for him to ignore his absolute and complete boredom with just about everything. Though his job had been going pretty well, he felt an emptiness that he could not replace. He accepted he could not play baseball anymore, but accepting it and finding a way to replace the thrill of competition and the feeling of being on a team were two different things. A while back, he had begun to think there might actually be some type of purpose in his life, but if so, he still couldn't figure out what that might be. Maybe now, at least for a while, things would be different. He hung up the phone and quickly called Emma and then Dylan to tell them his exciting news.

Dan attended the Tri-I Conference. The organizing committee had accepted his proposal to speak on the status of teacher compensation reform in the state. When Dan finished his presentation, he walked up North Fairbanks to Timothy O'Toole's, where he planned to meet Mike and take in some college football games on TV. Dan wore khaki pants and a navy sports jacket, and as he neared the bar, he took off his tie, tucked it in the inner pocket of his blazer, and fit right in. Dan and Mike didn't usually trek that far out, but with Dan in the area, and Timothy O'Toole's being his favorite stopping off place, they decided to make the trip. Suppressing the nagging memories of his visit there with Anna Jean was the one drawback of going there. Dan considered everything else about the place to be perfect.

Dan wanted to tell Mike the good news, but before he could, Mike, bursting with excitement, began to talk about a recruit who had committed during the recently completed early signing period.

"Dan, this guy is a stud. I can't figure out how we got him. Six-three, 200 pounds. I'm telling you, we're going to the College World Series if he doesn't get hurt. He throws ninety-three right now, with control. Three pitches. Right now. Give me one more class to put a couple guys around him. I'm telling you, Dan. I'm not kidding."

"Okay, I believe you, already. What's his name? Where is he from?"

Usually, Mike landed his share of good suburban players, managed to pull in a few junior college (JUCO) guys from the area, and, with his contacts, drew some players down from Wisconsin each year.

"His name is Tom Bickert. He's from Grand Haven, Michigan. I saw him play in a showcase tournament this summer. I sent him some information and followed up on it, and he said he'd heard of us from the regional last year. This fall, I gave him a token call, and he said he was interested. I assumed he was just saying that to appease me, but he visited, and things began to heat up. I couldn't believe it when he told me he was going to sign his letter of intent. I never talked about him before because I figured we had no chance. I mean, why the hell would he come here? This guy could go to Miami, anywhere."

"Maybe he wants to pitch as a freshman?"

"He'd do that anywhere in the country."

"Maybe he wants to be a number-one?"

"He'd be close to that at Miami, Texas, anywhere."

Maybe Mike might be around for a few more years after all. Though unlike Mike, Dan started to think he was exaggerating.

"Maybe he likes the city. How the hell do I know, Mike? Jeez. If he's that good, he'll sign in June, anyway. You won't see him."

"I know. I figure I'll lose him. Can't you give me a couple hours here before you shoot me down? Christ, Dan, I never noticed. Are your eyes ever blue." Mike was rambling a little. Dan wondered if he already had had a couple before Dan had gotten there.

"Jesus, Mike, you're not in love with me, are you? I couldn't take that."

"Well, it's just that I never noticed before. They twinkle."

"Stop it. I'm starting to worry about you. I'm not sure if I like you in this good a mood."

"You seem in a pretty good mood yourself. Talk go okay?"

"Well, it did, but I have other good news. Maybe not as good as you getting a commitment from Sandy Koufax, but pretty good news."

"Well, come on, then. What is it?"

Dan smiled a toothy grin and said, "Lindy called me this week. She said she got accepted to UIC, and she's coming to school here."

His current feeling of pure joy reminded him of when he had stepped on the Georgia campus for the first time the fall of 1992, twenty-two years earlier, when Anna Jean had said, "I think I'd like that," and when he had arrived in Chicago on the cusp of a new life seven years earlier. The feeling had a name—hope.

"What, you're kidding me?" Mike said. "I'm buying. Bartender!"

Dan and Mike originally had planned to head out early that day, watch some of the football games, get something to eat, and get back. But both were in such good moods, they lost track of time.

"Mike, isn't it about time to take 'er back?"

"Dan, the night is but a fetus."

They stayed, but Dan became wary. Like him, Mike had times of the year when he got a little melancholy, and the holidays were usually one of them. The longer they stayed, the more chance that the evening would take on a different tone.

So they BS'ed several hours away, talking about how great the next year would be, when finally, Mike asked, "Dan, what's it like, being a dad?"

"Well, I'm not sure I can answer that. I can't say as I've been much of one."

"Dan, your daughter thinks enough of you to come here. You must have done something right. You can't help everything that happened." Even when he had had a few, Mike knew better than to discuss Anna Jean. He had made that mistake once and took great care not to make it again."Yes, perhaps. Well, I don't know. It's like knowing things are about more than just you."

"I wish I had a family sometimes," Mike said. Then he called out, "Bartender, another one."

He turned to Dan. "It's your turn."

"I wanted to leave, and now you're ordering, and I'm paying?"

Mike seemed not to hear that.

"Mike, you have a family. What do you think you do in Appleton every Christmas?"

"You know that's not what I mean, Dan."

"Well, Mike, if that's what you want, then do something about it. They have girls in Chicago, last time I checked."

"Come on. I'm getting old. I don't have any money. I don't think I'd generate too much interest."

"That's not the impression I get every other weekend when I'm at home reading and you're out chasing."

"That's different, Dan. That's not what I'm talking about."

"Well, what are you talking about? Stop chasing women around and find someone to marry, if that's what you want."

"I don't know if I could do it. I'm recruiting all the time. We play all the time. I can't give up baseball."

"So, there are no other college baseball coaches in the country who are married?"

"Dan, I don't know if I could figure out how to even get along with anyone anymore. I don't think I'd know what to do. Women always kind of baffled me."

"You ever been in love? What about the high school girlfriend you always talk about? Whatever happened to her?"

Mike's face went blank. "I don't really know anymore. I've been a lot of different places."

"Sorry, man. You started it. I'm sorry. I'll stop."

"Dan, do you think I'll ever see him?"

"See who? Mike, you're not making sense anymore. Come on. Let's get the hell out of here."

"See my son."

Dan looked up at the ceiling exasperated. *Ey. Here we go again.* Dan assumed Mike had had too much to drink and must be confused about something. They'd been down this road before. Dan always knew better than Mike when it was time to shut it down, and the time had come to haul Mike's ass out of there. Dan did not feel like babysitting tonight. He wanted to enjoy the news of Lindy's decision. Dan looked back over to Mike, who sat motionless, staring at his half-filled glass. Then Mike gulped the rest of his beer, and Dan gave him the benefit of the doubt for just a moment and said, "What son? What the hell are you talking about?"

"My son. The one my high school girlfriend had my senior year in high school. The one we gave up."

"Jesus, Mike. What the hell?"

Then, the night got even longer. They continued to buy rounds, but reality seemed to sober them both up.

Finally, Dan said, "Mike, I think that maybe, instead of running all around the country chasing your dreams, you've been running away. I think that's why you keep chasing women around like you were Captain Kirk just recently beamed to Paradise Island. You're afraid. You're afraid of what might happen if someone actually likes you again."

That's when Mike said, "Dan, I think now it's time to go."

Dan didn't argue. The two did not talk about the matter again for a long, long time.

Mike woke up the next morning and felt like he had eaten a lot of chicken. Dan, too, for that matter.

Chapter 22

Ah, my friends from the prison, they ask unto me,
"How good, how good does it feel to be free?"
And I answer them most mysteriously,
"Are birds free from the chains of the skyway?"

--Bob Dylan
Ballad in Plain D

Dan spent a great deal of time planning for Lindy's arrival the upcoming fall. Dan had to help her coordinate her housing, registration, placement testing, etc. Due to Dan's employment at the college and her stepfather's income, they did not need to worry about financial aid. Lindy did not know exactly what subject she wanted to major in, but had been considering a profession in the medical field. UIC had strong programs in that area, which coincided well with her interest in going to school near her dad.

At the same time, Lindy still had her life in Georgia. She had the prom and graduation, which Dan flew down for. She had her AP tests to take and her senior softball season to complete. She had never looked to play sports beyond high school, partially because she knew her coursework in whatever medical-related major she eventually settled on would be extremely challenging.

Dan recalled how he had once wondered how he would talk with his daughter the first time she fell in love. Just exactly what would he say? Maybe she had thought she had been in love already at some instance for all he knew, but now, Dan was more than likely going to find an answer to that question somehow, someday, and maybe soon.

In the meantime, Mike went through what had become a rather typical season for the Flames: 32-26 against a tough schedule, a conference championship, and an early exit in the regional. Quietly, he hoped that his secret weapon would put them over the hump next year and feverishly recruited to find quality players to go along side Bickert. He landed him some better talent than normal, but he still only had so many scholarships to go around.

Mike held his breath the entire first week of June. The Texas Rangers drafted Bickert in the third round, and Mike thought for certain that he would sign. If he had been from an area more noted for baseball, Bickert might have even gone higher in the draft. Fortunately for Mike, Bickert's senior season was so-so. The pressure of having multiple sets of scouts' eyes lined up along the fence to watch him warm-up every single game would make it hard enough for most young men in his situation to perform. When the game started, the scouts would move from their position along the fence to a spot behind home plate, where each of them pointed their radar guns at him and jotted down notes that they steadfastly tried to hide from each other. They watched everything he did: the way he jogged to loosen up, his mental approach to his pre-game bullpen, and the expression on his face if he threw bad pitch. However, in addition to that, Tom's father had passed away from cancer in February just prior to the start of indoor practice, and while trying to impress his legions of admirers, Tom was trying to process all of the difficult emotions associated with his death.

Mike called and texted Bickert regularly in June, and Bickert continued to reassure him that he planned to come to UIC in the fall. Pro teams held the rights to a draft choice for one year, but once he attended his first day of classes, that player was committed to attend school, and at a four-year college, that meant he could not be eligible for the draft again until after his third year of eligibility. So, while Bickert was bound to attend UIC should he go to a Division I school, there was no guarantee—especially in Mike's world of paranoia—other than his word, that he was coming. The rules differed for junior college players. If Bickert wanted to, he could actually enroll in a JUCO program as a "draft and follow," pitch for a year, and sign before the next draft if he didn't like Texas's initial offer.

Time went by quickly, and before Dan knew it, Lindy had arrived in the second week of August and had moved into her room. Her mother and stepfather came up with her to assist with the transition.

Rarely were all of them together in the same place. Events like this and graduation notwithstanding, when Dan visited, he requested that her husband not be around when he picked up or dropped off Lindy. It might have been the year 2015, but Dan apparently lacked the sophistication that many others considered part of the times.

Anna Jean struck a stately and beautiful pose, on the one hand. She comported herself gracefully. Yet, Dan thought she moved rather stiffly and uncomfortably. She seemed stilted, almost stoic. Dan remembered her differently—soft, warm. Dan thought there could be any one of a number of reasons for this. She might have been sensitive to the awkwardness of the situation; she might not like the idea of Melinda Sue being so near to Dan; she might have disapproved of her choice to attend college in Chicago; or, perhaps some odd combination of all three, or even other things that Dan had not thought of.

Dan met them at the residence hall when they arrived.

"Good morning, Anna Jean, Dr. Taylor," Dan said, in a matter-of-fact, yet cordial manner. The doctor appeared to be about ten years older than Dan. He exhibited the type of attractiveness that money can buy. He exuded confidence, which to a stranger seemed nothing more than arrogance.

Dr. Taylor said, "Dr. Mason, very good to see you again."

"Dan, will be fine, if you don't mind."

Dan always called Anna Jean's husband Dr. Taylor out of respect, but also a childish refusal to acknowledge his actual name, Jay. Most doctors preferred to go by their first names in social situations, but Jay never bothered to correct Dan. People often believed the myth that educators wanted to be referred to as "doctor" at all times. Dan had repeatedly asked Jay to call him "Dan," but he would not, and Dan knew why. Dr. Taylor was mocking him, as if he wasn't a "real" doctor, which, in fact, Dan had never claimed to be.

Anna Jean tried to stay out of the middle of the two of them, and she, as much as Dan, also preferred they not be in the same place together whenever possible. When they were, she noticed the differences between the two, and she missed the man she originally married. She found it much easier to accept her current situation when she could more easily block out the memory of Dan. Dan had his faults, but when he and Jay were together in the same place, she noticed that Dan did his best to acquiesce to the situation, whereas Jay felt the need to go out of his way to belittle Dan. This bothered her. Earlier that spring, when Dan returned to Chicago after Melinda Sue's graduation, she stood up to Jay for the first time and said, "You, know, Jay, you don't have to be an ass to him to prove that you have me and he doesn't. Don't you think that's obvious enough to him?" After that exchange, she didn't talk to Jay for a day or so in fear that he might retaliate violently, either verbally or physically. He did not, that time, and during that twenty-four hour period of solitude, the stark contrast between the two, which she knew existed, became clear to her. It was actually very simple. Dan was a *decent* man, and Anna Jean wondered if, in some ways, his decency was what always made it so difficult for him to make sense of everything around him.

Melinda Sue and her mother had said goodbye. Anna Jean had sent her only child off to college, left her with her dad, and she and her husband had begun the trip back to Georgia. Only she knew if, on the inside, she felt as if she was actually returning "home." Anna Jean spent the trip back wondering what her life held for her now, and did in fact wonder how things might have been different. *What if Dan hadn't gotten hurt? What if she hadn't gotten pregnant? What if they had never gone back to Chicago? What if she hadn't lost the baby? What if she had the capacity to better express her love for Dan? What if, in an attempt to slow down her life to the pace she had grown up with, she hadn't gotten so scared and left him once and for all? In short, what if she hadn't been so damn practical about everything all the time and had allowed herself instead to soak up the carnival of human existence even just a little more? What if (gasp) she could have been just a little more like . . . Dan?*

But like Dan, she too was a product of her environment. As Dan had grown up with the Sears Tower in the background, he had developed a dynamic, wonder-filled outlook on life. Anna Jean had endured a static, mundane childhood. On top of it, her dad had left her to fend for herself. She had wanted something better than the Rayonier sawmill and the goddamn tedium of Swainsboro, and she did not want to be poor. Well, she had gotten something else, all right, and was she ever ill-prepared to handle it when it came to her. Over the last seven years, Anna Jean had come to believe that a life with Dan, or even a life in Swainsboro, would have been far preferable to her current supposedly "affluent" situation, and she hoped someday she could find the words to tell Dan she was sorry.

During those couple days in August of 2015, Dan couldn't help but think that Anna Jean did not come across as particularly happy (as he small-mindedly, secretly wished), but he would never know his perception was reality, or, if it was his over-active imagination trying to fashion a reality that made his loss easier to fathom.

While Dan had been welcoming Lindy and processing his latest encounter with his ex-wife, Tom Bickert also went through the same orientation activities, as his mother helped him move into his room. Unbelievably, according to Mike, he attended class on the first day.

That very night, Mike and Dan went out to celebrate their big day. They went to Timothy O'Toole's, the place they had first discussed the possibility of this miracle. The subject of Mike's fatherhood at age eighteen did not come up. On this night, both of them felt entirely too full of hope in the future to look back into the past.

At the conclusion of the first week of classes, on Sunday, after Lindy theoretically had finished studying, she and Dan took the train to Barrington to visit Emma. Dylan's family joined them.

Emma took one look at Lindy and said, "Melinda Sue, you have grown into quite a beautiful young woman. Every time I see you, you get prettier and prettier."

To herself, she thought, "My God, does she look like her mother." So much so that, the more Dan looked at her, the more he fell in love with Anna Jean all over again.

Chapter 23

I was so much older then
I'm younger than that now

--Bob Dylan
My Back Pages

Dan's life, like most of the rest of the world's, consisted of four seasons: fall ball, off-season conditioning, the regular season, and summer ball. Though he hadn't played in some time, Dan's neurons still made sense of his existence through the cycle of the baseball season. For the fortunate chosen few, their body clocks typically started around the middle of February with the four greatest words in the English language: "pitchers and catchers report"—a magical time of the year for all who loved the game. In mid-February of 2016, as the Cubs and the Sox traipsed off to Arizona for spring training, the Flames were about to embark on trip to Missouri to open their season.

They came back from Columbia with a 1-2 mark. Mike held Bickert back to start the third game. He lost a 4-2 decision, but pitched well in his debut.

Lindy achieved good grades the first semester—four "A's" and a "B." She was still considering becoming a doctor. She had to declare a major and didn't know exactly what she wanted to do, but as she became more acquainted with her options, she considered Microbiology and Immunology.

In the third week of March, the Flames were scheduled to open up Saturday at home against Valparaiso. Dan asked Lindy if she'd like to go to a game and stop by his apartment after. He suggested some baby back ribs on the grill. She consented.

They headed over to the field about one-half hour before game time. During warm ups, prior to finding a seat, they assumed Dan's customary spot and leaned against the fence along the right field foul line. They reminisced about the times she had come up in the summer and had seen her dad pitch on this very field, with the Willis Tower in the background. Dan also told her the story about the first time he had taken her mom to the city and how petrified she had been. Lindy had heard this story before more than once.

They watched the teams warming up. Bickert, not scheduled to pitch until Sunday, was running his warning tracks. The Flames were opening conference play, and Mike thought it best to keep the pressure off Bickert early in the season. Most of the team's followers believed that soon, and probably by the next series, he would be throwing the opener each weekend. As Bickert finished up his running and started back toward the dugout, he paused to acknowledge Dan. He had seen him before and knew he and Mike were friends.

"Hey, thanks for coming out. Nice day, eh, Doc?"

"It sure is. We're playing today. What could be better than that? Great day for the opener!"

"Who was that, Dad?"

"That's Tom Bickert. He's Mike's big recruit this year. He's scheduled to throw tomorrow."

"Oh."

They went to their seats and enjoyed the game.

After the game, they went back to Dan's place, and he started up the grill. Dan started talking about the barbecue sauce. Dan always looked for deals and usually bought some cheap brand or something on sale. But Lindy's presence made it a special occasion, and this time he had bought some Sweet Baby Ray's Honey Chipotle barbecue sauce and proceeded to explain to Lindy how much she would like it. She thought to herself, "*Dad, sometimes you are such a little kid. The things you get excited about.*"

They sat outside on this chilly day, relying on the sun to counterbalance April in Chicago.

"Do you need a sweatshirt or something, Lindy?" Dan always worried about her being cold.

"I'm fine, Dad. It's not the first time I've been to Chicago, you know."

Dan put on *Modern Times*. He was not about to push it, but slowly, he thought Lindy might come to appreciate the finest in music. They carried on a conversation as the smoke wafted around them, with Dan frequently commenting on how good it smelled. Dan noticed he had been drinking less lately. On this night, that didn't stop him from opening a Fat Tire, which had become his favorite beer.

"Lindy, I swear, you've grown up to be the absolute perfect girl—no thanks to me, of course."

"Dad, you know I'm not perfect. Nobody is. You think that because I'm your girl and you're happy to see me. I drove Mom crazy plenty. You just never saw it."

"Yes, well . . ."

Quickly, Lindy said, changing the subject, "But you can continue to think I'm perfect if you want."

"It's just, I imagined, well, this doesn't sound very nice, but I thought you might be kind of spoiled."

"I suppose maybe I am, a little. But, remember all those visits up here? Well, there were a lot of times that Grandma Emma would do things with me and take me places, and I think if anybody can keep you grounded, it's her. We would write letters and stay in touch. I learned a lot from her."

"Me, too."

"By the way, I know more about you than you think, Dad."

"Great."

"It's all good, Dad. It's all good."

Dan took the meat off the grill. He warmed up the bread, again explaining how much Lindy would like it, and they shared a meal together.

Dan had some work to do on Sunday. He had hoped to see Bickert throw, but that would have to wait. He didn't make it over to the park until the middle of the second game. However, one of the Mason's made it to the park to watch Bickert pitch and left after the first game ended. Lindy didn't tell her dad *everything*.

Chapter 24

And she said, "How are you Harry?"
I said, "How are you Sue?
Through the too many miles
and the too little smiles
I still remember you."

--Harry Chapin
Taxi

Lindy and her dad took in a few more games together, and Tom began to notice Lindy hanging around the park. He looked her up in the campus directory and asked her out on a date, and she agreed. They began to see each other a little more frequently, and, before long, Dan became aware of the situation.

"Dating a baseball player. That didn't work out too good for your mom."

"I'm not my mom."

Later that spring, Dan got a call from Mike.

"Hey, Dan, think you can call Duke for me?"

"Sure, I guess. Who we talking about?"

"Bickert."

"Bickert? Aren't you going to get him in a college league?"

"Well, all he'll do there is dominate a bunch of young guys who don't know what they're doing. At Lombard, he'll play against some experienced guys. That'll be better for him."

"You and I know that, but that's not the way it works anymore. They don't scout those leagues like they do the others."

"Dan, please quit telling me things I already know. Everyone knows who he is, and they'll make a point to see him. He wants to stay local this summer and take a few courses. He had to drop one this spring, and he wants to get back on track."

"You know that I know he's seeing Lindy. School might not be the only reason."

Dan liked Tom fine, but much as he loved his daughter, he knew it would be a mistake if she was the reason Tom wanted to stick around for the summer. If something went haywire, it would fall back on Lindy's shoulders, and what seemed like a good thing now, would have lasting consequences. For the good of *both* of them, Tom needed to make decisions at this stage based on what was best for him. Dan did not have enough information to really know Tom's motivation. Based on his experiences, this had disaster written all over it. While concerned for Tom's well-being, Dan had reservations due to his concern for Lindy. He did not want to see her hurt.

"Dan, you going to call?" Mike asked.

Despite his thoughts on the matter, Dan had also learned that one cannot control another, no matter how well-intentioned. If Tom wanted to stay in the area, he would find a way, and if Lindy had strong feelings for Tom, Dan's opinion on anything would be most irrelevant. Dan believed all he could do was communicate frequently with Lindy, know what was going on, and be there to comfort her if it all went to hell.

"Yeah, I'll call."

Dan called Duke. Tom played in Lombard, and Tom and Lindy fell in love that summer.

Shortly before Lindy's birthday in June, Dan's phone rang.

"Hello."

"Dan, I suppose you know Melinda Sue is dating a baseball player," said the unmistakable voice of Anna Jean.

"Yes, I know that."

Silence.

"And I said hello."

"Hello, Dan.

"Is she okay, Dan? I mean, is she doing okay?"

"Of course she is. Don't you talk to her? Her grades are great. She seems happy."

"How long has she been seeing this boy?"

"A couple months."

"Dan . . . what's he like? Is he a nice boy?"

"He seems like it. I don't know him that well. I haven't really spent much time with him, or anything, but he handles himself well. He seems like a pretty good guy. He's nineteen, for crying out loud, Anna Jean, and so is she. They're going to go through it all. We can't stop the hurt. Don't you think I would if I could?"

"Maybe it won't be like that, Dan."

"Well, I hope not."

"Dan, you have to talk to her."

"What's that supposed to mean? You can talk to her, too."

"I know, Dan, but you need to talk to her. She needs to know what she's getting into."

"Oh, Anna Jean, my goodness. I will talk to her, okay?"

"Dan?"

There was a pause.

"Yes, what? What do you want? Well?"

"Nothing. Just talk to her, okay?"

"Okay, I will," Dan said, followed by more silence.

"Well, goodbye, Dan."

And as she hung up the phone, eyes welled up, she did not hear Dan say goodbye, because she was busy saying, "I'm sorry." Quietly, under her breath, inaudibly, she said, "I'm sorry." That was all she could get out. Dan did not hear it.

"Goodbye. What was that? Anna Jean, did you say something?"

No one was on the other line.

For Lindy's birthday, Dan took her out to the Parthenon and told her stories about his boisterous childhood outings with his parents and his grandparents, and the raging arguments over who would pick up the check. Lindy had heard these stories before, too. To her credit, she understood her dad's subconscious need to try to jam eleven years into one and tolerated it well. Dan tried not to be too gregarious or domineering around her, but sometimes he went a little overboard, and when he did, she let it go. Lindy had a couple glasses of Roditas with her dad, and, at his urging, tried the Loin of Lamb.

"So, you and Tom are getting on pretty well?"

"Yes, Dad, we are."

"Does he treat you well?"

"He's very nice to me."

"Does he talk about pitching in the big leagues?"

"That's about all he talks about."

"What do you think of that?"

"I think it's great that he has a chance for something that terrific to maybe happen."

"Dad, you don't have to worry. I'm not my mom. I've told you that before."

"You know, Lindy, it's not you I'm worried about."

"What do you mean?"

"Lindy, you'll be fine. Do you know what a girl like you can do to a boy? Even a boy like Tom, who seems to have everything going for him?"

"Dad, I have no idea what you're talking about."

"I didn't think so. Look, let's just say this. Don't be surprised when you find out someday that he wants to feel like you love him more than he wants to pitch in the big leagues."

"Why does it have to be one or the other?"

"It doesn't, Lindy. It doesn't. But it might not always be easy, either."

"I think I might be falling in love with him, Dad. If I am, I promise to remember what you said."

Dan didn't say anything.

"Dad, think we can talk about something else?"

"Sure, how about Bob Dylan?"

"Well, okay."

"Hey, I'm joking. By the way, the next time you talk to your mom, tell her we talked, okay? She'll know what you mean."

Chapter 25

For you, there'll be no more crying,
For you, the sun will be shining,
And I feel that when I'm with you,
It's alright, I know its right

--Songbird
Fleetwood Mac

During their sophomore years at UIC, Tom and Lindy became inseparable. Lindy's grades continued to be strong, and Tom continued to progress well in the eyes of the scouts. At the end of that spring, Tom explained to Lindy that he was invited to pitch in the Cape Cod League that that summer

"I'm going to play for Falmouth," Tom said.

"Really? That's where my dad pitched."

"Your dad pitched in the Cape? At Falmouth? Wow. I didn't know he was that good."

"Oh, Tom," she kidded him. "You are such a superstar."

Embarrassed, he said, "That's not what I meant, but what a coincidence."

"They say he was pretty good. Can I come out and visit?"

"Would you really come see me?"

"Of course, I will."

"Falmouth!" Dan shouted when Lindy told him the news.

Lindy thought Dan seemed more excited than Tom. *Dad, you are such a little boy*, she thought again. When her dad got excited like this, his enthusiasm was infectious—contagious, and Lindy could only speculate that this must have been what had originally drawn her mother to him.

One night, shortly before Tom had to leave, he took Lindy out downtown for her birthday. They went to Gino's East for pizza, talked, and enjoyed a wonderful evening together. Both lamented having to separate temporarily, but Lindy supported Tom and knew how excited he was for the trip. They accepted that the next couple months might be difficult, but agreed they could do it. In addition to her visit, Lindy would be busy with summer classes.

"My dad always tells me how he took my mom here once," Lindy said. Then she asked, "So, Tom, do you like Coach Denison?"

"Sure. He's a good guy. He can't stop talking about the movie *Field of Dreams*, though. I mean, I like that movie, too, but he's just obsessed with it. I don't know how many times you have to watch a movie, but even *Caddyshack* fanatics haven't watched that movie as much as Coach has watched *Field of Dreams*."

"Tom, there's one thing I've always wanted to ask you," Lindy said.

"Well, go ahead."

"Why did you come to UIC? Nobody can figure that out. Everyone says you could pitch anywhere, and you were drafted so high. Nobody understands. Why did you come here? There must be a reason."

"Well, that's kind of a complicated story." He didn't seem too eager to tell.

"Well, we have time, Tom."

"Oh, boy. Well, here we go."

Tom's parents adopted him. They had told him that as a child, and he never thought of anyone as his dad except Mr. William Bickert, a plumber by trade. Still, as Tom grew older, he couldn't help but be curious about his real father and why he might have been given up for adoption. Tom's parents explained that his biological parents were very young and couldn't take care of him, but hearing that and trying to make sense of it were two different things.

The fall of his senior year, Tom turned eighteen. His biological father had signed a form stating that, when Tom turned eighteen, he could come to meet him if he wanted. Tom consternated over this for several months prior to his birthday. He wondered if his real father would be insulted if he elected to visit his biological father.

When Tom finally turned eighteen, he found the compulsion too strong, looked at the paperwork, and saw the name Mike Denison. *Mike Denison. Coach Denison. The Coach Denison, my father?* The Internet can be a marvelous thing, and as Tom read Mike's bio, he saw the words, "Appleton, Wisconsin native," and when he looked at his birth certificate, he saw the words, "St. Elizabeth Hospital, Appleton, Wisconsin," plain as day.

It didn't take too long for William to ascertain that the Mike Denison recruiting him was indeed Tom's father, but at no point did he ever let on to Tom that he knew. In fact, he couldn't have if he had wanted to. It would have to be up to Tom to pursue the journey back in time if he should so choose.

Then, in February, Tom's father died. Shortly before he died, he pulled Tom aside. Tom still had no idea that his dad knew that the Coach Denison recruiting him was the same Mike Denison listed on his birth certificate.

Under the guise of never having gone to college himself, Mr. Bickert said to his son, "Tom, I don't know how much longer I'm going to be around. It has to be your decision, but it sure would be nice if a Bickert boy would go to college. I don't know how the draft will go or anything, but I sure think UIC would be a nice place for you to go."

Tom relayed the story to Lindy.

"I realized he must have known. He knew it was bugging me. I came here because my dad encouraged me to come here and meet my real dad. I came for the same reason you did. I came here to be with my dad."

"Does Coach Denison know, Tom?"

"He doesn't know, and you have to promise me you won't tell anyone. You can't tell anyone."

Sometimes it's better not to ask questions.

"Promise me, Lindy."

"I promise."

Chapter 26

Make me an angel that flies from Montgom'ry
Make me a poster of an old rodeo
Just give me one thing that I can hold on to
To believe in this living is just a hard way to go

--John Prine
Angel from Montgomery

Lindy visited Tom in Falmouth. Needless to say, they enjoyed the visit. Like father, like daughter, or something like that. Fall came, and Lindy resumed her studies without skipping a beat, but Tom felt enormous pressure. With the draft looming and his personal situation unsettled, he appeared out of sorts and behaved erratically at times. While Lindy understood the situation, she had no way of truly knowing how he actually felt, and she knew even less how she might help him through it.

Dan could feel himself getting older, almost by the day. His feet hurt after a jog (of course, losing a couple pounds might have helped, but why go there?). His back bothered him frequently. He ambled up and down steps more slowly, and getting out of bed wasn't exactly the easiest thing to do, either. He thought, *When they put me in a cockroach-infested old folks' home, some Cook County care facility, will Lindy come to visit?*

Lindy went to Georgia for the holidays, but while Dan missed her, this time of year had taken on a special significance for him and his mom, which cushioned the blow of her absence. Dan always made arrangements for a special day with Lindy before she left, and each time, a certain awareness became more acute—their time together was growing short. Soon, she would move on with her own life, and there would be Dan, alone again. The followers of Flames baseball had been speculating, that, after this spring, when Tom would be drafted, Mike would likely leave for a different job. Dan never brought it up, but occasionally, Mike would mutter different things about new challenges and other code words for, "It's time to move on." Dan had begun to feel the familiar pang that, soon, he essentially would be starting all over, yet again.

This year, they had planned their celebration following Lindy's last final exam. They were making idle chatter and putting ornaments on the tree, when, all of a sudden, she said, "Dad, something's been bothering me."

"Shoot."

"Dad, have you ever broken a promise?"

"Notably, once."

"I'm not talking about that, Dad."

"Well, I don't suppose you live forty-three years without breaking a promise. I'm sure I have, at some point."

"Dad, Tom told me something, and I don't know what to do. I promised him I wouldn't tell, but I don't know if that's right or not."

"Your instincts are pretty good, Lindy. I'm not sure I can tell you what to do."

"Dad, you remember I told you Tom was adopted."

"Sure, I remember."

"Dad, Coach Denison is Tom's biological father. In a couple months, Tom will be drafted and gone. I suppose it's not my business, but the only reason Tom came here was to meet him. I think it's bothering him. I think he wants to tell him, but then, I think he's scared. Mike signed some form or something. I don't know what to do."

Dan looked down. "Well, Merry Christmas, eh kid?"

"You can't be mad at me."

Dan notice that she was fighting back tears and went to hold her. "I'm not mad at you, but this is—this is—well, I don't know what this is. I don't know if it's our business. I don't know what to do. He told you this? Jeez. I tell you what, I have to consult someone way smarter than me. I will talk to grandma next week."

"You say he told Melinda Sue?" Emma said.

"Yes."

"And Mike told you he gave up a son when he was eighteen?"

"Yes."

"Well, don't you suppose there's a reason they both told someone else? How would you like to carry something like that around with you your whole life? They need help, Dan."

"Well, what am I supposed to do? How am I supposed to do anything? What if I screw this up? This is monumental."

Then, it occurred to Dan. Finally, he thought he had found his purpose in life. As Jessica Carter had done for him, now Dan must do for another. He would pay her favor forward. It was his turn to play angel. Selfishly, he thought, *maybe I just found my idea for that book that's been eluding me.*

Chapter 27

I was sitting in the bathtub counting my toes,
when the radiator broke, water all froze.
I got stuck in the ice without my clothes,
naked as the eyes of a clown.
I was crying ice cubes hoping I'd croak,
when the sun come through the window, the ice all broke.
I stood up and laughed thought it was a joke

That's the way that the world goes 'round.

That's the way that the world goes 'round.
You're up one day and the next you're down.
It's half an inch of water and you think you're gonna drown.
That's the way that the world goes 'round.

--John Prine
That's the Way That the World Goes Round

The spring of 2018 was upon them, and once again, the Flames, and everyone else around the country, had begun to enjoy the crack of the bat.

Lindy and her dad had spoken several times since the holidays, and of course she often brought up the issue of Tom and Mike. Once, she said, "Dad, we're running out of time!"

"Lindy, I know we need to do something. I just don't know what."

"Well, think of something!"

Tom got off to a tremendous start. His stock continued to climb, and rumors that he might even go in the first round began to circulate. Plenty of Flames had been drafted over the years, but the only UIC player ever to make it to the major leagues had been Curtis Granderson, who had ironically played for the Tigers, the team that had drafted Dan eons ago. Spring was disappearing rapidly, and Dan would have to think of something.

During the second weekend of April, UIC hosted Youngstown State. Tom threw well in the opener. Once the season started, Mike's schedule did not allow for much of a social life, but Dan and Mike managed to find a day here and there to hang out for a while, and Dan suggested they visit Timothy O'Toole's, their new and favorite stomping grounds, after the game. Mike thought that sounded like a good idea, and after the double-header sweep, it sounded even better, and off they went.

They engaged in familiar baseball banter about the game, who did what, why, what they should have done, how that sets up the next day, etc., and while that could have gone on forever, with both of them happy, Dan finally said, "Mike, you know, you told me what happened when you were a senior in high school, you and your girlfriend and the baby?"

"Yeah, I remember, Dan."

"Would you want to see him?"

"Hell, I got nothing to lose. It's not up to me. Would he want to see me? That's the question."

"So you would, then, do you think?"

"I suppose. I suppose it could either be good or one of those things where you just have to get it over with, but I think, sure. I'd like him, maybe—though he probably could never love me—to see that I am human. That I fucked up. That I'm just a guy, not the devil."

"Yeah, so tell me, think Tommy can get you out of the regional this year?"

"Actually, yes. I think we're going to the Super Regionals."

Sixty-four teams qualified for the NCAA Tournament for baseball, divided into sixteen, four-team Regionals. Those teams played a double-elimination tournament, and the remaining sixteen teams were paired off in a best-of-three matchup, with the eight series' winners going to the College World Series. UIC's record currently stood at seventeen wins against eight losses.

They headed back fairly early that evening, and bright and early

Sunday morning, Lindy called Dan and asked him the same question she had been asking him for months.

"Did you talk to Coach Denison?"

"Yes. I talked to Mike last night. He would see his son, if he had the chance."

"Well, what do we do now?"

"I haven't gotten that far yet."

Then, Lindy, unbeknownst to her dad, decided to take matters into her own hands.

Monday evening, after practice, as he frequently did, Tom walked over to Lindy's apartment. After a few minutes, Lindy blurted out, "Tom, please don't hate me."

"Hate you? I love you!"

"Tom, I broke my promise. I told my dad about Mike being your biological father."

"You what?"

"Tom, why do you think you came here? Do you want to leave no better off then when you came? Once you leave, you may never get the chance again. It might be gone."

"Lindy . . ."

"Tom," she interrupted, "I did it because I love you. If I really screwed up, then you can hate me forever. After I told him, I learned that my dad already knew Mike had a son when he was eighteen. He asked him if he would be willing to see you, and he said he would. He still doesn't know it's you. It's no different than before. Everything is still up to you."

Tom walked around in circles, thoroughly confused. Everything was coming to a head. Lindy didn't know what to expect from him next. She thought he might leave. If he did, she thought he might not come back. She even thought, for just a second, that he might hit her. Lindy saw Jay do that to her mom, once. Tom looked in the freezer. "I want a pizza. Do you have a pizza?"

"I think so. Take whatever you want."

Tom started to pre-heat the oven, grabbed a beer, and then sat down on the couch next to Lindy.

"Dammit, Lindy, sometimes you drive me crazy."

He didn't say anything for a while. Finally, he spoke again. "Lindy, please, please don't ever leave me. I don't know what I'd do."

And then she moved over to him like she had done many times before, and they sat. Later, he ate a pizza. Lindy had no idea what would happen next.

UIC plowed through the conference tournament, and, for the first time in school history, won the Regional. In the Super Regional, North Carolina took two of three from the Flames, ending their season. Tom won the first game, but UIC lost the next two. The Flames finished the season with a stellar 46-18 record. Shortly thereafter, Mike announced that he had accepted the coaching position at the University of Tennessee.

On June 5th, Lindy turned twenty-one. Dan called her a couple days prior.

"Lindy, I suppose you have better things to do, but do you suppose it might be possible that, on June 5th, you stop out for a couple with your dad before I turn you loose on the town?"

"Dad, I never thought you'd ask. As I look, it appears that my schedule will allow for that."

They went to Timothy O'Toole's. As they walked down the steps, Lindy said, "Dad, I know that you came in here with mom, once," and they both laughed.

A few days later, the general manager of the San Francisco Giants called Tom to inform him that they drafted him in the first round, eighth overall. Tom immediately dialed Lindy's number.

"Lindy, the Giants took me. They picked me eighth, Lindy! Eighth!"

"That's wonderful! Can I come over to celebrate with you?"

"I'm going to call my mom and then run over to the field and see if I can catch Coach real quick. I'll get in touch when I get back."

Lindy hung up the phone and called her dad to tell him the news.

"Is he over there now?" Dan asked.

"No, he said he was going to the field and he'd get back with me in a little bit," she replied.

"I'll be by in a minute. Be ready. We'll meet him over there and surprise him," Dan said.

Tom knew Mike would be at the field. Many teams rented the field over the summer, and somebody had reserved it for that evening. Mike went down there in the afternoons to get the field ready, take the tarp off the mound, open up the gates and the press box, and turn on the scoreboard. He may have accepted another job, but that would not keep him from going to the field every day. Mike knew of no other place to be, and Tom, like everyone else, knew that. Mike hadn't turned his keys in yet. Until he did, odds were, you'd find him at the field.

Sure enough, when Tom got there, he saw Mike tamping down the mound area.

Tom dropped a small duffle bag to the ground as he entered the gate. Mike heard the noise and looked up.

"Hey, Tom, you got news?"

"I do. The Giants took me—first round."

"No shit?"

"No shit!"

"Wow. That's unbelievable."

They did not say anything for a while.

"Well, grab a rake anyway," Mike said.

"I suppose the university will have to retire your number and all that to get you to give them some money," Mike said.

"What money? I haven't signed yet."

"Oh, whatever."

About that time, Dan and Lindy pulled into the parking lot. As they got out of their car, they saw the two talking.

"Maybe we better stay here," Lindy said.

"Yeah, I think you're right."

So they stood there and watched.

Mike and Tom puttered around on the field for a bit and finally, Tom said, "Hey, Coach, you know, you've been like a father to me."

"Oh, come on, now. A brother, maybe. How old do you think I am? You know, we never would have gotten out of the regional, and I never would have had a chance at the Tennessee job, if you hadn't come here."

"Don't mention it, Coach. You earned it. I enjoyed my time here."

It was time to water down the mound.

"Get the hose, Tom."

"Wait a minute."

"Okay, but we're running out of time."

Tom trotted back to the fence, zipped open the bag, and took out two gloves and a baseball.

"What are you doing?" Mike yelled.

Tom returned to the field, handed one of the gloves to Mike, and uttered the penultimate line from *Field of Dreams*. "Hey, Dad, wanna have a catch?"

Mike stared at him in disbelief. He looked at him, and looked at him, and looked at him some more. *It can't be. He's bigger than me. He doesn't act like me. He doesn't look like me at all. But nobody would be so cruel to pull this kind of a prank. It must be true! Tom Bickert is the boy I gave up twenty-one years ago! My "son," sort of anyway, was just drafted in the first round! He played for me! Most dads coach their sons at some point. I can say I coached my son!*

Mike thought there would be plenty of time to talk some more if that was what Tom wanted. They couldn't fit these complicated things into a five-minute initial meeting. *Don't ruin the moment. Make it last.* Mike could think of only one thing to say.

"I'd like that."

Soon after, Mike left for Tennessee and Tom signed a contract with a $5.7 million signing bonus. The Giants assigned Tom to the South Atlantic League—Augusta, Georgia, to be exact—where he would start out with the Augusta GreenJackets. Lindy visited her mom and Tom in Georgia and returned for her senior year of college. Dan prepared for her eventual departure and got to work on his book. He thought he might have something this time. He had an idea bouncing around in his head about dreams, fathers and their children, and maybe a little baseball and Bob Dylan for effect.

There seemed a certain order to things, but in reality, everything was just as uncertain for all of them as it ever had been. *Who knows,* Dan thought, *maybe I might even fall in love again?*